The Best of CaféLit 8

The Best of CaféLit 8

an anthology

Edited by Gill James

Chapeltown Books

British Library Cataloguing in Publication Data

A Record of this Publication is available from the British
Library

ISBN 978-1-910542-45-3

This edition published 2019 by Chapeltown Books
Manchester, England

All Chapeltown books are published on paper derived from
sustainable resources.

Contents

Writer's Choice

We asked those writers who were published in *The Best of CaféLit 7* to vote for their five favourite stories published on the CaféLit web site in 2018. We awarded five points for number one choices, four for number two and so on.

The following stories received votes and are listed in the order of receiving the most votes.

Authors were not allowed to vote for their own stories. It's quite a tall order, anyway, to ask people to read all the stories published in one year but a few did and these are the results.

Next year, for *The Best of CaféLit 9*, we'll ask those who appear in this volume to vote. We'll allow them five votes for each story they have had published.

We have a volume of about 30,000 words which is exactly right for a *Best of CaféLit*. This produces a respectable book that has a nice spine but is also one that retails at a reasonable price.

Salisbury Plain, February 1946

Laura Gray

Manhattan Sour

In the empty theatre, the moth-eaten velvet curtain jerked slowly upwards. A lone man sat at a table on the brightly lit stage. White coat over his olive army uniform, stethoscope round his neck. A clipboard and a small torch held upright completed the props. His form was silhouetted and magnified against the backdrop, the stark light of the spots giving it an air of menace.

In the wings what could have been a clutch of chorus girls pressed together, awaiting their entrance. Ranging in age from sixteen to thirty, naked under identical bathrobes with 'Property of US Army Tidworth' stencilled on the back.

"Well, I suppose I am," giggled Marjorie, just eighteen and looking nervous. Eleanor stared straight ahead.

Two Red Cross nurses were attempting to herd them into a queue, with limited success. In exasperation, one of them barked: "You want to be on that ship to New York next week, right?" Nods from the women. "You want to see those Yanks who've been fool enough to marry you?" Emphatic nods, indignant glares. "Well, you have to have a medical, and this is it. Now, who's first?"

A brief silence, then Eleanor stepped forward. Since this was a stage, she would use her extensive experience of Miss Holcombe's PE class to play the part of a shy teenager stepping into the communal showers, faking bravado to get through the ordeal. She strode up to the table, chin up, waiting until the doctor raised his head and met her eyes. "Name, please."

"Eleanor Mary Snyder."

A mark on the clipboard. "Open your robe, please, and step your feet apart."

Eleanor remained unflinching while the torch probed under her arms and shone between her legs. "Thank you, that's all." She forced her shaking knees to carry her into the wings on the other side of the stage, where clothes were piled in a row. She retrieved her soft cotton dress, lovingly made by her sister. Annie had used her own coupons to make sure Eleanor had 'something nice to travel in'.

That was the medical. The rest of the women, watching Eleanor, turned to each other in disbelief. "What's he looking for?" hissed Marjorie.

"Sores," said one woman.

"Crabs," said another. None the wiser, Marjorie took her turn. As she stood straddling the worn floorboards, the doctor motioned to the Red Cross nurse. A whispered conversation, and Marjorie, crying and protesting, was led away towards one of the cast dressing rooms.

Silenced, the rest of the women strode the stage in turn, and then dressed with relief. As the group left the theatre, a notice board proclaimed:

TIDWORTH THEATRE FILM NIGHT
THURSDAY 8PM
MAIN FEATURE: "FANNY BY GASLIGHT"

They stared. Then one by one, they doubled over, faces running with tears of uncontrollable laughter.

When they boarded the Queen Mary the following Thursday, Marjorie was nowhere to be seen.

About the author
Laura Gray enjoys attempting short stories and the occasional poem. Most of all, she is enjoying putting together a book based on the experiences of a World War II GI Bride.

No Room for Them

Dawn Knox

Sherry

Midnight Mass was over.

Shortly, the congregation would reassemble for the Christmas Morning service but now, the vicar surveyed his festive church with its twinkling Christmas tree, and Nativity scene. Earlier, candles had glowed in the darkness as carols echoed from its ancient walls.

The house of God is such a beautiful place, the vicar thought.

Locking the church door securely, he made his way home, turning his face from the rows of people lying side by side in shop doorways, swaddled in blankets and cardboard.

It never crossed his mind God would want them to sleep in His house.

About the author

Dawn's first success was with a short horror story published in a charity anthology entitled *Shrouded by Darkness* in 2006.

Several years later, she had a Young Adult book (*Daffodil and the Thin Place*) and a single author anthology of speculative fiction stories (*Extraordinary*), published as well as several historical romances, set mainly during and between the two world wars.

She has written two plays about the First World War, one of

which commemorated the beginning of the war and was first performed in England in 2014 and then in France and Germany. The other play commemorated the end of the war and was performed in England in 2018 and in Germany 2019.

Using her World War One research, she has also written a book entitled *The Great War – One Hundred Stories of One Hundred Words Honouring Those Who Lived and Died One Hundred Years Ago* which was shortlisted for the Wishing Shelf Book Awards 2018, a finalist in the Readers' Favorite Book Awards 2018 and a finalist in the Independent Author Network Awards 2018.

She has written short stories for several women's magazines as well as pocket novels for My Weekly Magazine.

She Says We'll Get There Soon She Says
Hannah Retallick

Hot chocolate

Mummy says we are pilgrims. Pilgrims are people who go off on an adventure to some place special and they hardly ever cry because they are brave. Brave people are sad too, I say, aren't they? They are, she says, but sometimes it's better not to show it.

It isn't a nice time for pilgriming. It's dark – she's whizzing around my room, picking up my things, throwing them into her red spotted backpack with the breaking straps, which makes me worry about Bob. Bob has been squished in and might get bruised like Mummy. Mummy fell down the stairs yesterday and it made a lumpy sound, but she didn't scream or anything and she smiled at me after, so I know she was okay. Okay enough for Daddy not to come down.

Down the stairs now, carefully, quietly, she says. Says Grandma will have Maltesers. Maltesers are what we're going for and we're going in the night so that when we get back we can surprise Daddy. Daddy isn't one of the pilgrims. Pilgrims need to be girls or teddy bears, says Mummy.

Mummy strangles my hand, pulls me out onto the dark street with scary shadows – now, walk quickly Jenny, I can't carry you. You will get more sweeties at Grandma's if you are quick. Quick is hard when you're sleepy, everything is hard when you're sleepy – that's why I cried before.

Before we had got to the end of the street, I told Mummy she was hurting, stop please. Please keep moving, don't drag your feet, she says, we'll get there soon, she says. Says when the pilgrims get scared they—

Daddy's coming. Coming faster than we're going – he's cross, like when I was bad and left Bob in his doorway and he's using the same words. Words he hit me with.

With one arm, Mummy pushes me behind, turns, raising the other arm in front of her. Her grip stops my fingers feeling – I press my head onto her long red coat, push my nose right into it. It smells of good.

Mummy?

About the author
Hannah Retallick is a twenty-five-year-old from Anglesey, North Wales. She was home-educated and then studied with the Open University, graduating with a First-class honours degree, BA in Humanities with Creative Writing and Music, and is studying for an MA in Creative Writing. She is working on her second novel and writes short stories and a blog. She was shortlisted in the Writing Awards at the Scottish Mental Health Arts Festival 2019, the Cambridge Short Story Prize, and the Henshaw Short Story Competition June 2019.

https://ihaveanideablog.wordpress.com/

Jeopardy in Pink

Penny Dale

Bloody Mary

The wipers lazily cleared rain from the windscreen of the big Mercedes. Ruslan left the motor running, she'd find out soon enough that he had guessed what she was up to and he didn't care if she saw him in the square. In fact he didn't care about much, except for money all of the time and for sex and cocaine on a sometime basis.

The doors of *Exquisite by Allia* opened and Luisa emerged. When she'd asked him if she could do some shopping and have some beauty treatments he'd agreed. He liked her looking good; he was going to do some business in Panama in a few days. Her looks could be very useful.

Then she'd said, "Darling, would you mind if I'm late home? I'd like to go and see my mother."

At the time he was distracted, concluding a deal with the Venezuelan security services. There was a lot of money involved and he didn't trust them. He'd nodded, "Don't be too late."

Later, the deal completed and the money safe in a Swiss bank account, Ruslan considered the sudden mention of Luisa's mother. They'd been together for eight months and she'd never once alluded to any family, let alone her mother living in the same city.

His suspicious mind started working. What was she up to? Who was she meeting?

It wouldn't hurt to keep an eye on her.

It was easy to watch her cross the square. Her magenta umbrella bobbed above her head, undulating slightly as her high heels accommodated the uneven cobbles. In the gloomy afternoon rain it shone like a beacon, lighting up the grey square and protecting Luisa's lovely face and immaculate hair from the weather.

She was heading towards the district where there were lots of bars and restaurants.

"Her mother won't live there" Ruslan snarled to his empty car. "She's meeting someone." He banged his fist on the steering wheel and began to think about what he'd do when she got home. He must be careful; he wanted her to look good for Panama.

His sadistic fantasies were halted by the realisation that the bright umbrella had stopped in the far corner of the square. Every day of the week and in all weathers a youngish man was there selling flowers. He did good business especially in sunny weather and on days when there was a wedding in the Town Hall. Ruslan briefly recalled his own sham marriage. Flowers, an obligatory kiss for the photograph and then his bride – what was her name? – whisked away forever.

Ruslan watched as the flower seller left his stall

and walked towards the now distant umbrella. He appeared to be carrying a large bouquet of pink roses.

"So what the hell are you doing leaving your pitch? Don't you know there are criminals about?" He smirked and watched with increasing rage as the man handed over the flowers and gave Louisa a brief hug. As far as Ruslan could see, no money changed hands. He saw the man return to his flowers and the two-timing Luisa vanish into the steady rain, swallowed up by the hurrying crowd.

Out of Ruslan's sight on the other side of the square Luisa was glad of the shelter of her umbrella. She wished she'd had some time to talk to her brother, they rarely saw each other. She didn't want her unpredictable lover to know anything about her family. It was safer for them if he didn't even know they existed. She'd had to tell him about her mother, otherwise he'd have been suspicious when she was late back from the salon. His controlling jealousy was frightening, but he could be generous, especially when she was 'nice' to his business contacts. Luisa had debts to clear, so she went along with his demands and irascible temper.

She pulled the umbrella closer to her head and reached into her bag, fumbling for her phone. Balancing bag, umbrella, roses and phone wasn't easy but she managed a brief text. "Sylvie gave me roses for Papa; we'll go to the cemetery together. Ruslan knows I'll be late."

Dry inside his Mercedes a red mist gripped Ruslan. No one cheated on him and got away with it. He revved the engine hard, reversed without even a glance in his mirror and accelerated the wrong way down a one-way street. The two-timing bitch deserved all that was coming to her. He'd find another babe to take to Panama. That gaudy umbrella wouldn't be any protection from what he had in mind.

About the author
To celebrate her 70th birthday this year, Penny has published a selection of her writing *Enjoying the Ride*. The book contains published and unpublished short stories, poetry, flash fiction, a play, a blog post, even some academic writing! So far voluntary donations amounting to almost £400 for copies of the book have been sent to Versus Arthritis.

penny49@uwclub.net

Marking Time

Janet Howson

Christmas punch

The tree lights could be put on, the main light was too harsh. The cards were festooned around the room alternating between garish primary colours, sparkling, snowy scenes and the comical ones. She received a lot of cards, well over a hundred, but then again she sent a lot. Every year she meant to cut down as the cost of stamps was getting ridiculous, but she never did. Presents were balanced one on top of the other all wrapped painstakingly in the same or similar paper, displaying an identifying gift tag for ease of identification. The turkey had already been put in the oven and it was starting its considerable journey on a very low heat to its eventual destination on the dinner table. She had already peeled and cut up the potatoes, parsnips, carrots and broccoli and as an afterthought, put some peas in a pan. The gravy couldn't be done until the last minute but she had already put the cranberry sauce in a glass dish. She didn't bother with bread sauce anymore. Year after year it would return to the kitchen, untouched. Her mother was bringing a microwaveable Christmas pudding and she had cream and brandy sauce in the fridge.

All was prepared but she had this task. A task she

must complete before the rest of the household appeared. She had put it off too long. She didn't want it hanging over her head like the Sword of Damocles, spoiling her day, not to mention the rest of the holiday. No, it had to be done. Why not today? It was, after all just another morning and those who would disapprove would not be up for hours yet.

She sized up the considerable pile of blue exercise books. Some were pristine, some rather grubby and a few without their cover. She picked up her register to enable her to record the marks. She uncapped her red pen.

She sighed at the inevitability of the task.

It was marking time.

About the Author

Janet taught Drama and English for 35 years, directing a lot of plays, some of which she wrote herself. She has been spurred to start writing again having found a folder of poetry she had written over the years. She is now enjoying writing short stories with the aim of turning some of them into scripts. She feels as if she is at the start of an adventure and feels very excited about it.

Rose Tinted Glasses

Linda Payne

Mock champagne

Aah, my two lovely boys, Nick and Sean. I'm looking forward to seeing them today. Just waiting for my girl Rachel then we can go in together.

Nick's dad was tall, dark and handsome. He takes after his dad.

Sean's dad was smooth, smart, sophisticated and when my boy flutters his eyelids he looks just like his dad, or at least I think they both take after their dads. I mean how well do you remember people after a few drinks on a one-night stand?

I remember Rachel's dad well enough though. He hadn't long come out of prison and, well, you know how it is, every man needs his comforts now and again so I just comforted him. In fact, I comforted him a few times.

He did do the honourable thing though; he did offer to marry me when he heard I was pregnant but when I learned that he murdered his second wife that put me off a bit. They don't know what happened to his first wife. Hasn't been seen for years. She seems to have disappeared somewhere. Probably doesn't want the attention.

Why I'm visiting my two lovely lads in prison I don't know, I mean take Sean for example, so he was caught with his hands in the till. I reckon that if they'd paid proper wages instead of this zero hours nonsense he wouldn't have done it. Treat people well and they're okay. Alright, so he wasn't working for the company he stole from at the time, but he might have been.

And then there's Nick, I mean what millionaire surrounds their houses with razor wire? My poor Nick didn't stand a chance when he slipped and fell on it. Scarred him for life that has. He was only trying to help some old lady get her cat back.

Caring and considerate is my Nick. Anyway the shotgun he was carrying didn't belong to him. He was looking after it for a mate. He didn't know it was loaded when he shot that policeman in the leg.

I just think the policeman held a grudge. My boy wouldn't hurt anyone on purpose. That policeman had it in for him, all the police had it in for both my boys. That's the only reason they're both in prison. Very kind-hearted boys, my lads.

Take Sean, he spent a whole morning collecting money for the wheelchair that the policeman now needs and what thanks did he get for that? None. I remember that night he took us all out for dinner, it was at a posh restaurant up west. He said he'd treat us all to a celebratory meal for his having raised so much money. Bought me a lovely outfit from Harrods for the occasion.

Everyone's always picked on my two boys ever since they were in the juniors. All the local shopkeepers banned them from their shops. Said my boys were stealing. Why tempt kids with interesting stuff and put them where kids can easily reach them? That's only asking for trouble.

Okay the boys had to go to the back of the counter for the fags, but I blame the shopkeeper for that, he should have served my boys instead of answering his landline. Only had himself to blame, should've used a mobile. My boys are good boys; they are always looking after their mum.

As does my daughter, Rachel. Good girl she is. The neighbours say she is cheap, they even went so far as to say that she is a bit of a tart. They're only jealous. One nasty old crow said my Rach earns her money at sex parties. I told her straight I said if my girl can earn enough money to pay for a penthouse and a Ferrari by selling frilly knickers to people in their own homes it just shows what a good saleswoman she is. That shut her up. I can tell you.

Only a couple of minutes to go. I hope Rachael won't be much longer. Oh good here she comes. Cutting it a bit fine but never mind she's here now that's all that matters. We can go and visit her brothers now.

About the author
Linda has been writing seriously in the past few years before then she was just a hobby writer. She enjoys writing monologues and has won prizes for them. This is the first that she has submitted to Café Lit and she feels very proud of its inclusion in the anthology.

Remembrance Day

Jim Bates

Elderflower cordial

"Allie, come here, a minute. Look at this." the old man said and pointed. "It's a special kind of wild flower called a trillium."

Intrigued, the little girl ran to his side and fell to her knees, her face only inches from the white petals.

"Pretty," she said, and bent closer to smell.

"There's usually not much of an aroma," the old man said, as he stiffly got down on the ground, joining his granddaughter.

"But, Grandpa, I can smell it," she said, excitedly, moving over to make room for him, "You smell. It smells good."

He bent down and took a whiff of the imaginary scent. "Oh, you were right," he said, looking with affection at a little girl, "I can smell it now. It does smell good."

They were just coming out of a small woodland near the park where they'd been playing on the swings. A moving shadow on the ground caught their attention. The little girl looked up and spied a large bird.

"Crow," she dutifully recited. The old man grinned with the memory of when he'd taught her to not only identify the bird, but also say its name. Then a sudden movement on the ground to the left captured her attention. She turned quickly and saw a robin hoping nearby on a sunlit patch of grass. "Look at that," she said, pointing excitedly, "Rrrr… rrrr… Robin." She looked at her grandfather and smiled. It was their little joke about how he'd taught her to identify this particular early spring bird and pronounce its name with r's for both robin and red breast.

God, the affection he felt toward this little girl, the youngest of his son's four kids.

Suddenly, nearby, a dog yipped. Allie stood up quickly and pointed, "Look Grandpa. A doggy."

He stiffly got to his feet and turned. Coming down the street was a lady in a blue sweat suit walking a small white dog that was straining on its leash. "Stand behind me," he said to Allie, and moved her out of the way, protecting her. As the lady approached, he said politely, "Nice dog you've got there. What kind is it?"

She gave him an odd look, sizing him up before answering, "It's a Westie."

He turned to his granddaughter, "Did you hear that? Can you say 'Westie', honey?"

Allie didn't answer, only watched shyly as the lady and the dog walked by, hurrying a little, it seemed to the old man. He watched until they were out of range and then asked, "Did you like the doggy?"

"I did, Grandpa, I did. He was so cute," she exclaimed, smiling. "I loved it."

"Maybe someday your mom and dad can get you a doggy," he said, starting to walk down the street toward his son's home.

She reached up and took his hand. "Maybe," she said, doubtfully. Then she had a thought and visibly cheered, "But, if they don't, will you get one for me, Grandpa? Please?"

He smiled to himself before answering. "Well, it's really up to your mom and dad." Then he glanced at her, and, seeing the disappointment in her eyes, quickly added, "But, we'll see, sweetheart. We'll see."

"Good," she said, smiling. Then she started humming to herself. The old man didn't recognize the tune, but that was alright; it was just good to be together. They walked along for half a block, taking their time, until Allie let go of his hand and pointed, "Look Grandpa, tulips," she called out, "Come with me. Hurry." She ran ahead to the next yard.

The old man followed behind, his steps slow but steady. In a minute he caught up to her. She was squatting down, studying the bright spring flower. "Two, two, two lips," he said, pointing to his mouth as he approached her.

She turned and laughed. "No, Grandpa. Tu…lips," she said, emphasizing each of the two syllables. He smiled, remembering how much fun it had been teaching her letters and words throughout her young life. She moved over to a different flower. "Look Grandpa, your favorite color. Orange."

"Yes, it is, honey." Then he paused and rubbed the whiskers on his chin in mock contemplation, "Say, what's your favorite color again?" he asked, pretending he'd forgotten.

"Purple and pink," she said, standing up and poking at him. "You know that." She giggled and then added, "You're so silly, Grandpa.

They started walking again, her soft, small hand in his large, callused one. She was five years old, average height, and was way too skinny in his estimation, even though she ate like a horse at every meal. She was fun loving and had a unique personality all her own. Her mother let her dress however she wanted and, today, she was wearing yellow and red striped tights under a white and black striped short-sleeved dress covered with pink hearts. On her feet were purple socks and pink tennis shoes. Her long red hair fell past her shoulders and freckles dotted her checks. When they were together they talked and laughed and she was a true joy in his life.

The next house up ahead was his son's home. He pointed, "Let's go into your folks' back yard and play."

"Sure," she agreed and ran off, the old man following as fast as he could, which wasn't saying much. He was eighty-six years old and wasn't getting any younger.

A few minutes later his son Steve, who was standing at the window and looking into the backyard, called to his wife, "There he is. I see him. There's Dad."

"Finally," she said, somewhat annoyed. "He's lived with us for ten years. Today of all days he should know we'd be eating by six o'clock."

Steve checked his wristwatch and said, "He still has a few minutes."

"What's he doing out there anyway?"

"Looks like he's dancing."

"What?"

"Dancing." Steve shook his head grinned to himself. He liked that his father was a bit of an eccentric. It kept things interesting. Most of the time, anyway, but not today. Today different. "Never mind. I'll go get him."

"Please hurry. I'm putting the food on the table."

In the dining room were Steve and Emma's other three kids and their four young children. This was the family's Remembrance Day. The day they set aside every year to remember the short life of Alisha Ann Drayton, Steve and Emma's youngest daughter, who fifteen years ago today had died at the age of five from acute lymphoblastic leukemia.

Steve went downstairs and out the back door. "Hey Dad," he called, "come on in. Dinner's on the table."

Out in the yard, the old man stopped running around and playing tag with Allie. She was wearing him out and he was getting tired. He wasn't as young as he used to be.

29

He turned toward his son, "Alright. Just give me a minute."

"Sure, Dad," Steve said, walking over. He put his arm affectionately around his father's shoulder, "You doing okay?"

"Yeah, son, I am." He was quiet for a moment, "I just miss her, you know. I miss being with her. Playing with her. We were close. She was one of the best things that ever happened to me." He paused a moment and then added, "It's not just today, son, but every day. Every day is Remembrance Day. At least it is for me." His eyes suddenly became moist as tears formed.

Steve sighed and gave his dad a compassionate hug. "Me, too, Dad," he said, "Me, too."

Then they walked slowly toward the back door. The old man didn't want to go inside just yet, but knew he had to. Emma had dinner ready and he didn't want to be rude. After all, it was generous of his son and wife to have him live with them. More than generous.

Over his shoulder the old man turned and waved to Allie, standing in the middle of the yard. The wind blew through her hair and the sun caught her freckles just right, making them seem to sparkle. She smiled at her granddad and waved back, locked forever in the old man's memory.

"I'll see you soon," he said to his granddaughter as he turned and started for the door.

"What'd you say, Dad?" Steve asked.

"Nothing," the old man said. "It must have been the wind."

Then he turned and waved to Allie one more time before finally going inside.

About the author

Jim lives in the small town of Long Lake, Minnesota, twenty miles west of Minneapolis. In 2011 he began devoting much of his time to writing: firstly, poems, haiku and ditties which he self-published. Since 2015 he has switched his focus to fiction: short stories, flash fiction and micro fiction. In March 2018 he began to send his stories out to try to reach a wider audience. His first story, *Remembrance Day*, was accepted that month by CaféLit and he has since become a regular contributor.

In addition to CaféLit his stories have been posted on-line at *Paragraph Planet*, *The Writers' Cafe Magazine*, *Cabinet of Heed*, *Ariel Chart*, *Potato Soup Journal*, *Nailpolish Stories* and *The Drabble*, and published by *A Million Ways* (an Indie Publication), and *Mused – The BellaOnline Literary Review*. He also has a blog where he regularly posts his stories:
www.theviewfromlonglake.wordpress.com

Yellowjackets

Jim Bates

Black coffee

It was Field Day, the last day of school for the Long Lake fifth graders. I was looking forward to tomorrow: no kids, no schedules, no rules to enforce. No nothing. I was also looking forward to a summer of alone time – my idea of heaven.

I was standing on the sidelines, monitoring a soccer game between my class and the other fifth grade class, Mrs. Elbert's, and talking to Edith Silverstein, the oldest teacher at the school. She was a sixty-five year old, outspoken, dynamo of a woman who had taught first grade for nearly forty years. Lots of people thought she should retire because of her age. Not me. She was a witty lady with a great sense of humour who had a firm but gentle and kind way with children. I liked her a lot.

"What are you planning on doing with your summer, Randy?" she asked, both of us idly watching all ten kids on the field run after the soccer ball.

"Oh, nothing much. Just hang around. You know."

She bristled in response like I'd just poked her with a sharp stick, "No, I don't know, young man," she spat out. "You should do something meaningful with your summer other than just 'Hang around'."

32

She used finger quotes to make her point. Then she shook her head in semi-serious disappointment, letting me cogitate on her words, making me feel like a properly chastised pupil in her class. She had a way about her, I'll tell you.

After the moment passed, she smiled and changed the subject, "Me, I'm going on a month long cruise to Alaska with my friends Maggie and Becky. I can't wait." She gave me a look like, 'See. Us old people can have fun. Get with the program and do something interesting with your life.' A sentiment that made perfect sense, especially after what was about to happen.

I'm forty-five, a bit of a loner and have been single my entire adult life. I live with my big tabby cat Toby in a tiny apartment a mile from the school, close enough to walk or ride my bicycle. Long Lake is small town located on the edge of undeveloped farm fields and woodlands twenty miles west of Minneapolis. I've taught fifth grade Life Science in the local grade school for the last twenty-one years. Although I'm withdrawn by nature, I love teaching. It's just that it takes a lot out of me. I treasured my time to myself, but understood what Edith was getting at and valued her opinion. When I really thought about it, at my age, maybe I really did need to do something more interesting with my free time than pursuing the only hobby I had, collecting vintage dinky toys off eBay.

Anyway, her analysis of my life notwithstanding, we'd been having a nice, friendly conversation when from the far end of the soccer pitch we heard screams from the kids. "What the hell?" I turned to Edith.

She yelled, "Go," and I did. I took off running wondering what had happened.

I soon found out. Both fifth grade classes were standing where the soccer field met the woods. The kids were yelling as I ran up, some even crying.

Johnny Leibert, one of my prized students met me, "Mr. Mack, Mr. Mack. Shelly's getting attacked by bees. I think they're going to kill her."

The Shelly he was referring to was Shelly Goldenstein, a ten year old tiny waif of a girl, prone to hives and every other kind of skin problem you could name. She was also the unluckiest kid I ever knew. Last year she kindly brought her teacher a handpicked bouquet of wild flowers that included a sprig of poison ivy. She was covered in calamine lotion for nearly a month. If anyone was going to be attacked by bees or wasps or any other kind of stinging, biting insect, it was bound to be her.

I ran to the edge of the woods as Shelly frantically waved the attacking swarm away from her face. I could see in an instant that they weren't your common, ordinary, garden variety honey bees. No. These were wasps, more specifically yellowjackets, one of nature's most vicious, predatory insects. They could sting you multiple times and really do some serious damage. I'd read once that their stingers felt like hot needles pushed deep into your skin. My heart went out the little girl and I didn't stop to think.

"Shelly, Shelly," I called, "Don't worry, I'm coming." I ran in to rescue her.

She turned, tears in her eyes, those angry yellowjackets swarming all around her, crawling on her arms and legs and face, stinging at will. "Help me, Mr. Mack, please, help…" she called except it wasn't as much a call as it was more of a whimper. She was really frightened. Terrified. Poor little kid.

I picked her up and swung her in a circle a few times to try to shake some of the wasps off. As I did, I could see what had happened. The soccer ball lay next to a log rotting on the forest floor. The kids must have kicked the ball into the woods and Shelly had run in after it. The ball had hit the log and disturbed their hive. By the time she got there she was met with the wrath of what seemed like hundreds upon hundreds of raging yellowjackets.

I held her close to protect her and brushed away as many of the wasps as I could. Then I ran to the edge of the woods, where I yelled at the rest of the kids, "Get the hell out of here. The wasps are coming." They ran and I did, too, a full out sprint of a hundred yards back to the school, all of us out running the yellowjackets easily. In about a minute we were all safe.

Fast forward to two hours later. It turned out that

Shelly was going to be okay, just a little swollen around the ten spots where'd she been stung. Me? I ended in the hospital – the Hennepin County Medical Center. Unbeknownst to me, I had developed an allergy to wasp and bee stings over the course of my adult years. I'd had no idea. But it turned out to be a blessing in disguise even though I was told by the doctors and the nurses many times over that I'd almost died. I'd been stung twenty-seven times. Those yellowjacket stings threw me into anaphylactic shock, my throat constricted and my blood pressure dropped off the chart. It was adrenalin that got me from the woods to the school where I collapsed in the bushes by the front door. In short, I was lucky to be alive.

Recovering in the hospital for three days gave me a chance to think about what Edith had said to me on the soccer field; you know, about doing something meaningful with my life other than just hanging around my apartment. After all, I had come close to dying from those yellowjacket stings. I came to the conclusion I really did need to get my act together; I needed to expand my horizons.

To that end, just before I was released I accepted an offer Edith made to join her and her friends on their Alaskan adventure. It might sound weird, me, a guy in his forties going on a cruise ship with three elderly ladies, who, by the way, call themselves, "The Girls," but I don't care. I'm looking forward to it.

When I accepted the invitation Edith said, "You're an okay guy, Randy, and it'll be nice to have you along, just don't go cramping our style."

"Funny," I told her, playing along, "I'll try not to."

She gave me a mischievous grin, and didn't say anything more. We're leaving the first week in July, and I think it'll be fun. I have a feeling I've got a lot to learn. By the way, Shelly's going to take care of Toby.

You know, when you almost die, like I did, it gets you thinking. I won't bore you with all the details, but I will tell you this: If it wasn't for those swarming yellowjackets, I might have ended up spending the summer hunkered down in my tiny apartment with my cat, searching the internet for old dinky toys. When I think of it that way, I shudder. I was on path where I could have easily spent the rest of my life doing just that, becoming more and more of a recluse. What a waste. I've got a lot to learn about life. It's a big world out there and I'm looking forward to seeing it. Alaska, here I come; me and my EpiPen.

About the author
Jim lives in the small town of Long Lake, Minnesota, twenty miles west of Minneapolis. He enjoys walking, gardening, bird watching, reading, writing, bicycle riding and being with his grandchildren. For many years he worked as a sales and technical development and training instructor for a large manufacturing company, and most recently was part owner of a small gift shop near to where

he lives. He collects old marbles, vintage Dinky Toy race cars, YA books from the 1900s and vintage radios from the 30s and 40s.

In addition to CaféLit his stories have been posted on-line at *Paragraph Planet, The Writers' Cafe Magazine, Cabinet of Heed, Ariel Chart, Potato Soup Journal, Nailpolish Stories* and *The Drabble,* and published by *A Million Ways* (an Indie Publication), and *Mused – The BellaOnline Literary Review.* He also has a blog where he regularly posts his stories: www.theviewfromlonglake.wordpress.com

God Works in Mysterious Ways Especially at Christmas

Robin Wrigley

Mulled wine

In 1973 I was working on the fringes of the Sahara in Algeria. We were camped less than an hour's drive south from the small town of Messaad, east of the main provincial town Laghouat. It was necessary to pass through Messaad to access the main road to either Laghouat or Algiers.

It wasn't long before we discovered that a group from the British charity 'Save the Children' were based in an old French fort in the town and we went to visit them and say hello. The manager was a retired army officer and the medical staff comprised two mid-wives and a lady doctor. We quickly established a friendship and always called in whenever we had occasion to pass by. The staff liked to see fellow countrymen dropping in and we became very useful to the group in being able take mail for them or help out with supplies. For us it was a welcome watering point on journeys out of the desert, especially if it coincided with a meal time.

A few weeks before Christmas that year I was scheduled to make a two-week break in England. On my way up to Algiers I called in at the charity and collected their Christmas cards and wish-lists of things they wanted buying for them in London. It was arranged I would make various purchases and also contact the doctor's sister to collect her presents to carry back.

Little did I know what I was letting myself in for with this offer, now becoming purchaser and carrier. Most of the items requested were from Marks and Spenser's ladies underwear department! The doctor's sister's gifts took up a quarter of my suitcase and the assorted purchase items another quarter. The other half was filled with various Christmas goodies such as mince pies, Christmas cake and pudding. Thankfully I did not need much room for my own personal effects.

The next hurdle was the Algerian customs authorities at Algiers airport. The country was still coming to terms with the dreadful and prolonged war of independence, and the treatment of foreigners was not very friendly. Baggage searches were very thorough and nit-picking. Magazines zealously scrutinized for any racy photos or anything likely to offend good Moslem conduct. Advertisements for ladies underwear would result in the page being ripped out or the magazine completely confiscated.

The large amount of ladies underwear in my bag caused considerable concern but I lied explaining it was for members of my family. The rest of the presents and Christmas goodies survived the check.

On Christmas day the five of us who were left on the crew arranged a 'service day' and finished around midday, washed, changed into our best available clothes and headed north to Messaad. Their manager was not present having arranged to go home to England for the holiday, but the doctor and midwives had entered into the spirit with decorations, mince pies and mulled wine.

They had also wrapped presents for each of us and although the gifts were simple and really no more than tokens we made a big scene of opening each one with cries of surprise followed by much applause. My present was a pair of M&S socks. Sad to say it was the sum total of my Christmas presents that year.

We then retired to the dining table where a fine seasonal feast had been laid out; what with that and the local wine we wanted for nothing even though we were far from our homeland.

After the meal we played the usual silly games, sang Christmas carols and generally chatted and reminisced about our lives and our families. Later in the evening after another snacking type meal we bade our hosts farewell and set off into a cold but clear Saharan night on our journey back to our camp.

Our camp life continued much the same as ever

until three days before New Year I received instructions from Algiers head office that we should strike camp and head to a new concession further south and then east near the town of Touggourt and on to a camp site in El Oued, a date-growing area. The preparations for the move made it impossible to bid farewell to the charity. It wasn't until after the dust settled and the camp reorganised that I discovered my Christmas present of the socks was missing, presumed stolen.

Not long after this move I became disenchanted with the new area, the company management, the flies in the date growing oasis and life in general and I resigned and returned to London.

Since my time in Algeria I have worked and lived in many countries worldwide but at this time of the year I often reflect on the loss of those socks. Did the thief enjoy them? I consoled myself with the thought that he probably needed them more than I did.

A few weeks before Christmas in 2017 a package arrived for me from a company called 'Bamboo' of whom I had never heard before. Inside the package was a very nice pair of blue-striped socks, just my size.

This year the same thing happened again! God really does move in mysterious ways.

About the author
Robin, a relative newcomer to short story writing, has spent the majority of his adult life as a land surveyor and

later a country manager working in over twenty countries world-wide. The variety of the situations he has faced and the people he has met inspired him to create many of his stories. His stories have been featured both on line and in print with CaféLit as well as two other short story collections. He is a member of the Wimborne Writers' Group.

Goodbye, My Lush...

Shawn Klimek

Sloe gin, at high speed

Her dress was askew. Her hair looked like a tumbleweed flattened by a truck.

She had slipped down off her seat and was groping drunkenly for the dashboard.

Goodbye, my lush, I thought bitterly. *I'm leaving you.* We had both been drinking, but tomorrow – as usual – only I would remember.

As I prepared to leave, my heart ached and it got harder to breathe. *I still loved her.*

Then I saw a puddle pooling at her feet, staining her skirt.

To hell with this, I decided.

Taking a deep breath, I kicked out a window and swam for the surface.

About the author
@shawnmklimekauthor/facebook

Losing Tony

Gill James

Earl Grey tea

The clock on the church tower has just chimed two. She said she would be here at three. Lunch was over and done with at one. Even the dish washer was loaded. And now it has run. It's too early to unload it. Yet I can't settle to anything else. Will she be on time? I don't know. I don't know her at all. Is she like me? Does she waste a huge portion of her life being much too early for fear of being late? I don't even know whether I want her to arrive ahead of time, so that we can get it over with, or late so that I've got more time to get myself ready.

My stomach churns. Can I keep my lunch down? Will I be able to offer her tea and will we get round to eating the cake? Is it stupid to offer tea and cake on an occasion like this? At least the weather is warm. We can sit in the garden. Being outside always makes things seem better doesn't it?

She'll be a complete stranger, won't she? I've not met her before. Just that one time in a dream. When she was six or so and she'd managed to swim a length of the school swimming pool. I was standing holding a towel for her. Out of the water she came. Athletic and strong and at the same time so feminine and completely my little girl.

Now I can feel my own heart beating wildly and the hall clock ticking. They're in harmony. They are both counting my life away.

I think of the last time I saw Tony. It was a day just like this. We walked down to the corner shop to buy some ice cream. His idea and his treat. As usual I had to trot at his side like a pet dog. He eats well and he's a good cook. He remains thin because he's he walks everywhere and so fast. It's hard to keep up with him.

He's always been a bit of an enigma, my son, my first born. Yes he's tall and strong. Years of dancing, ice-skating as well as the fast walking have made him muscular and supple. He can be strong. He's got back up after blow upon blow. Yet he can cry buckets about a sad film or the death of an animal. He is so talented and creative – and messy. Out of chaos comes beauty.

He daydreamed as we ate the ice cream. It was as if he wanted to tell me something but couldn't quite get round to it. I knew, though, when he left that day we would never see him again. He confirmed this later by phone. And no, we've not seen him since. Not for over three months. We mourn him. He is gone from us. Forever.

I decide I must look my best to meet my unknown daughter. I'm glad I had my hair bleached white. It doesn't make me look old – quite the opposite. I'm sure Tony would have confirmed this and certainly his younger sister approves.

"Just, think, Mum, you could have purple streaks put in. Tony would have loved that," she says.

Yes I'm sure he would. Well at least I can go for purple eye shadow but I stick to a more conventional lipstick shade. Who knows what she'll be into?

I decide I can't slop around in my jeans. I must be smart even if I look casual. I select a top in my best green and my beige linen trousers. Will it do? If only I could ask Tony. He was always good at helping me to find the right clothes. I got that promotion when he chose the bright pink suit for the interview. That white linen skirt he found the day he got the job at Selfridge's lasted for years. And what about those high boots he picked out when we went on the day trip to France? I wish I could ask him now.

I look at the mugs and plates I've set out and decide they're wrong. I open the china cabinet and get out our best tea set. This is an occasion. We must treasure it.

Seconds after the church clock chimes quarter to the hour I hear the clatter of heels on the footpath. I brace myself for the doorbell. I don't have to wait long. My mouth is dry as I make my way to the door. I see the silhouette of a very tall person through the frosted glass. It could almost be Tony. I am trembling so much that I can hardly open the door.

I manage at last and there she is. Soft blond curls

frame her angular face. She is wearing a short shift dress in my green. What about that then. Size six, I would say. Size six for goodness sake. Well, at least she won't be stealing my clothes like Tony used to steal his father's. Her make-up is immaculate. Subtle. You can't really see it's there. A small patent leather bag hangs from her shoulder. Under her arm she is carrying what I recognise as a painting. It is wrapped in brown paper. She hands it to me. "This is for you. You might like to get it framed."

She slips off her jacket and sits down at the dining table as if she's been coming here for years.

I open the packet. I recognise one of my book covers.

"Thank you," I say.

She nods and looks down at the table. "Oh you've got the best china out."

"Well it's a bit of an occasion, isn't it?"

She shrugs. "What's the cake?"

"Raisin parkin." I remember how much Tony used to like it.

She grins. Her face crinkles and her eyes are just like Tony's.

We chat. It's as if we've known each other for years.

Then though there is an awkward silence. She puts her hand on my arm. "Should we go round to that picture-framers you told me about? I could help you chose something."

"That's a nice idea."

It's less than a mile away but it's too hot to walk. We take the car. We can't stop right outside. The primary school is emptying and lots of mums have come in cars. We have to park about four hundred yards away.

We set off.

She strides ahead. The heels don't faze her. I have to trot along, just like I did with Tony.

She pauses and turns. "Come on, Mum."

The sun catches her hair. She looks really pretty. My lovely daughter Toni.

About the author

Gill James writes fiction for all ages. She also works as a publisher and creative writing lecturer.

Her latest novel, *Girl in a Smart Uniform*, the third in the Schellberg Cycle, is published by Chapeltown.

Self Assessment

Peppy Barlow

Double espresso

Rosemary is sitting in the doctor's surgery. He is a very personable young man, she thinks. Not tall dark and handsome but he'd do. He's twisting a pencil in the fingers of his right hand. Not looking at her.

Outside there is a man working in the garden. He has dark hair and a colourful waistcoat. A large pair of sheers in his hands. He is pruning with abandon. He reminds her of someone but she can't see his face. What's wrong with her today? Eighty four and still eyeing up the talent.

The doctor is saying something. She must pay attention.

"Did you hear what I said?"

"Not really, no. I was somewhere else."

"Yes, well, that often happens. That's why I wanted you to have someone with you."

She hadn't thought to bring anyone. Only children need someone to take them to the doctor. "Did you say I was going to die?"

"Something like that, but not yet, maybe not at all. You can never be sure."

"I think that's probably something we can all be sure of."

"Well, yes, ultimately but you know what I mean."

"I do."

Now he is looking hard at her. Trying to hold her gaze. Are they trained for this, she wonders? Are they told you must look a dying person in the eye? He looks so young and vulnerable. She wants to get up and put her arms round him. She doesn't.

"How long do you give me exactly?"

"I can't be exact."

"Roughly, then. I'd like to know what I have time for. Have I time to go on holiday? Time to throw a party?"

He looks away. The pencil is on the move again. "Six months, a year, maybe more. Could be a matter of weeks. It's difficult to predict."

"Then I'd better go home and sort things out."

He looks up. "There are other avenues we could explore, experimental programmes."

She watches as the man in the garden cuts the head off a rose. She smiles. "No, doctor. Don't you worry yourself about me. You've done your best. And, I hate to tell you this, but one day you are going to die and no one will be able to save you."

She gets up to leave. The pencil stops moving. As she shuts the door he turns to his computer and puts the pencil down.

And now she is nearly home. She turns her small car into the street. Stops by the house she's lived in for the past thirty years. Gets out and goes to the door. A small black cat comes round the house to greet her. Rubs himself against her leg. She looks down.

"I should have taken you with me. He wanted me to have a friend."

She unlocks the door. There is post on the mat. She picks it up and moves down the hallway. There is a gallery of family photos on the wall. Pictures of herself as a child, her parents, her brothers and sisters, her children, her grandchildren. She stops at a photo of a man standing beside a vintage sports car. Taps it and speaks.

"Not long now, you old villain. You better not have another woman with you when I get there. You hear me."

She moves to the kitchen. Puts on a kettle. Drops a tea bag in a mug. Goes to the table and looks at the post. Mostly junk mail. A postcard from a friend in Greece on holiday. She glances at it. *Think you'd like this place. Lots of drink and dancing. Come with me next time. Sue.* Also a letter from the Inland Revenue. She opens it. It is a self-assessment form.

"Good lord. Do they really know what they're asking?"

She makes her tea and sits at the table with the form. The cat jumps on her lap. She strokes him. Talks to him. "Now let's see, what do they want to know? I was good at school. Did quite well really. Went to university. Fell in love more times than I can count now. Only one man really mattered but then you don't know that until afterwards. Couple of kids. Don't think I was a very good mother but they seem to be alright so perhaps I didn't do too much harm there. Sometimes remember my grandchildren's birthdays. Sometimes take them to the sea and let them run wild. Isn't that what a grandmother is supposed to do? Bit of travelling. Bit of teaching. May have had some affect. Not very nice to my parents I don't think but don't suppose they noticed. Or if they did they probably blamed themselves. Isn't that how it works? Plenty of people I would like to have slapped at the time but that's all gone now. We all harbour hidden resentments which mean nothing to the other person. I wonder if this is what they want. And which part of the form to put it on? Wonder what my friends would say about me? Is there a section for that as well? Somebody to speak up for me…"

The doorbell rings. She puts her mug down. Goes to the door. The man from the doctor's garden is standing outside. The man from the photograph.

"Oh, didn't expect you just yet. Haven't finished filling in the form."

He smiles. She reaches for her coat.

"I hope you know the ropes… Must admit I was a bit rattled when he told me… but there we are… nice of you to turn up…"

The man stands back to let her pass. The vintage sports car is parked in the drive. Rosemary laughs.

"You're not still driving that flash car. God, will you never grow up?"

The door closes. The cat mews and moves to the closed door. We hear the car start up and move off. The cat turns. Moves back into the kitchen where Rosemary's body is slumped over the table.

About the author

Peppy Barlow is a founder member of The Woven Theatre Company and a lecturer in Creative Writing at the Ipswich Institute. Her latest work is a site-specific play at Landguard Fort in Felixstowe on the life of Philip Thicknesse, Governor of the Fort 1753-66.

www.woventheatre.co.uk

Years and Years

Kim Martins

Vanilla cappuccino

Yes, it was him. He walked into the Red Oak Café and, for a fleeting moment, she thought he had spotted her tucked away in the corner by the window. She preferred the obscurity of corners filled with fake flowers and checkered tablecloths. She sipped the froth of her vanilla cappuccino (with an extra shot and a dollop of cream).

They had met in the cafe years ago, when it was called the Lygon, and the oak tree in the outside courtyard was as lanky as they were. They sat together at this same window table where she listened to the heartbeat of her future. But she learned that rushed promises are not always kept.

His hair was thinner now and his waistline fuller. He carried himself with that same steely confidence.

A woman with long, peppery hair waved to him from a table near the cake counter. She wasn't the type Peggy thought he'd go for. Chunky silver rings and organic colours. She probably ordered a decaf soy latte and ignored the carrot cake (with cream cheese frosting).

He threaded his way towards her. Their smiles connected. Warm cheeks pressed together.

Peggy pulled out an old newspaper clipping she

kept in her purse and looked at the grainy photo of a younger man. The clipping read: "Bob Templeton. Missing. Beloved husband of Peggy. Last seen Christchurch. May 10, 1996. Reward."

She ordered another vanilla cappuccino (with lashings of cream) and tasted the sweet deceit.

About the author

Kim Martins lives in New Zealand and is a travel writer and editor for the *Ancient History Encyclopedia* (www.ancient.eu). Writing has always been an important part of her life. She writes short stories, flash fiction and poetry. She won a flash fiction contest in 2019 and her poetry received Highly Commended in an international poetry contest. Kim's writing has been featured in Barren Magazine, NZ Poetry Journal, The Copperfield Review, Flash Frontier, Furtive Dalliance Literary Review, New Reader Magazine, Fewer Than 500, Plum Tree Tavern, University of Iowa anthology *The Brave & The Afraid*, and CaféLit.

Airport Sandwiches

Pat Jourdan

Tea with sugar

Margo turned up early at her father's house at the edge of Johannesburg without much luggage. Stan was surprised how much she had changed after her divorce, but then it was quite a while ago. They sat outside on the veranda in the evenings planning his visit to his brother in Montreal, a last chance to meet as they were both in their late seventies. Margo had persuaded him and even suggested going with him as encouragement.

"It'll be a wonderful thing to do, meeting after twenty years! You'll both be so glad and you'll wonder why it took so long – Uncle Oscar will be really pleased you made the effort!" Margo cheered him up. She set to work on her laptop, finding out flight times, connections, printing out tickets and boarding passes, comparing currency dealers, travel insurance, looking for somewhere to stay overnight in Montreal and ordering new suitcases. "At least you've got a ten-year passport already, or we'd be stuck here waiting," she added.

"It's a good job you went to that conference in Canberra after you retired. We'll need visas for Canada too."

Stan was impressed how business-like his daughter

was, how capable. She even organised new clothes for him, taking him with her and seeing that he bought outfits that would impress his brother.

"I'll just dash off to the travel agents now about the visas while you try on something warm for Canada wear." Margo was like a whirlwind.

They managed to get through Johannesburg airport with the least trouble.

"We're on our way at last!" Stan said, a bit relieved it was really happening.

In Stansted airport Stan sat watching the people opposite, sitting in the brightly lit café that served real meals. He could see families sitting down to large plates with hot dinners, set next to desserts and drinks. Drifts of assorted food aromas reached him. Perhaps later he could go across and manage to have something to eat, but he had to ration out his money to last until tomorrow. All the other outlets were coffee bars, sandwich shops, newsagents, money-changers and boutiques selling all kinds of luxury goods. The never-ending stream of passengers entertained him; or at least they had at first. Now it was getting later, five in the afternoon here, something like eight o'clock in the morning in his jet-lagged bloodstream.

He still could not work out how Margo had happened to go off with his passport and his tickets. She also had most of his money as he had packed his jacket and only had a little space in his waistcoat pockets.

"I'll take care of all that, Dad," Margo had said. "I've got this handbag. After all it's more convenient if I carry the lot together. And you shouldn't be carrying so much loose cash, you might lose it." She kept pointing out how forgetful he was these days, and she was right. Ever since she had come to stay she remarked how often he could not remember where he put things and how his memory was really befuddled. Often he was puzzled at this; living alone, he had not noticed it until Margo had come to stay. Suddenly he was losing keys, forgetting to lock doors, mistaking the right time; it was a catalogue of mishaps. As she emphasised, all the more reason to go and visit his only brother while he could still manage the journey.

It had taken some courage to go and contact the enquiry desk and ask about the two o'clock flight to Montreal. But the check-in clerk could not help.

"That's gone several minutes ago. It's up on the board, you can see it on the Departures section," the assistant pointed out. "If you did not turn up on time there would have been a public announcement. Didn't you hear it?"

Stan was sure he had not heard his own name called but these days he was becoming more doubtful day by day.

"I've been here in the departures hall all the time, heard nothing at all. You say the flight has gone? My daughter's on it, she has my passport and the tickets too." He did not mention the money, the precious rands changed into Canadian dollars.

"Her mobile won't be working while she's on the flight, I suppose, so it's useless trying to get into contact until they land." The enquiry assistant looked at him carefully and being both kindly and efficient, made a call to Montreal arrivals hall that Ms Margo Naidoo, flying from Johannesburg via Stansted, should be contacted as soon as possible to come to their passenger counter and produce her father's passport and tickets to the authorities in Canada.

"Well, that's all we can do so far. You'll be able to do something about that tomorrow morning. I'm sorry, that's as much as we can do at present. You see, right now you have no confirmed travel identity and you cannot buy another ticket without your passport or credit card. We have to wait until we have confirmation."

She looked over the passenger details of the flight again, but could find no entry for any Stan Govender. "Are you sure this was the right flight? There is another one later this evening. It has to have a changeover in Reykjavik 19.30 and arrives at Pierre Trudeau International the next day – you'll have quite a wait, unfortunately" But that flight was also without any trace of his name. While Stan waited for any news he had time to think and wonder. How had Margo been separated from him in the luggage hall?

He had been waiting for her at the carousel for

60

their suitcases and she had been lost in the crowd. He wheeled the overladen trolley into the airport hall, thinking Margo had probably gone off to the toilets but she had not reappeared. Stan loitered at the arrivals concourse along with all the taxi drivers and tour representatives. Nearly an hour had gone by before he accepted that something had gone seriously wrong. He did not have enough money to go off to a nearby hotel now, either – Stansted had several in the grounds. Margo had taken his wallet, for security, she said. "I'll keep all the important things together, Dad, so you don't lose anything."

He sat with the trolley piled up with Margo's and his own suitcases, sure that the mess would all be settled in the morning.

Getting into conversation with a middle-aged woman at the next table as they sat outside a café, Stan told her he was stranded here because his daughter had gone off to Montreal with his ticket and passport. He was stuck overnight with nowhere to stay. "I'm just going to sit here, have to sleep in a chair, she'll be getting in touch as soon as they land and the mix-up can be settled. Just got to last the night here," he said.

The woman was worried, though, and went across to a security attendant nearby, telling him of the old man's plight. "He's not a youngster and he can't be left alone in an airport all night sitting in a plastic seat. In fact he doesn't look at all healthy to me. I'd help, but my own flight to Vienna is due soon and I've got to be off."

"I'll have a word with him. You mean that old guy over there by Pret A Manger with the gigantic luggage trolley? We have little overnight cabins for situations like this, anyone ill or overnight staff having to stay. Don't worry, we'll look after him."

She went off to the take-away café and came back with teas and large sandwiches of cheese and tomato in wholemeal bread. "It's the healthiest version I could find. I don't know if you take sugar. There's two sachets here," she said as she sat down next to him again. "I love these airport sandwiches. I wonder where they get this bread from. Is it something special? It tastes so different from any at home." Stan accepted the tribute of food gratefully.

He had not realised how out-of-pocket he was. A few rand still in his pocket; not enough for a meal in any currency. It occurred to him that in this quickly-moving crowd he could sit here unnoticed as the world walked past. No one would see him.

The attendant showed Stan into a cabin, explaining he would be called for at first light. He would be safe in the forest of cabins until the morning. "Yes, this one is called 'Larch.' They're all called after trees, Birch, Oak, Ash, Fir, Holly, Rowan, Willow and so on – they're all here." He helped Stan wheel the luggage into the little cabin and left Stan sitting on the bed. He was worn out and beginning to be far more worried now than he had been earlier. Bits of questions were falling into a strange jigsaw. Opening one of Margo's three large cases, he found it full of old books; another was full of shoes. In her other case there were no clothes, no toiletries, just newspapers and magazines. It was the luggage of a woman who was going to disappear.

About the author
Winner of the Molly Keane Short Story Award and runner-up in the Michael McLaverty Short Story Award. She has published three novels, plus collections of poetry and of short stories. She is also an artist, with the next novel named *A Hundred Views of NW3*.

Budgies and Bingo

Alyson Faye

Earl Grey tea

Pulling up outside Aunty Elsie's terraced house, we all pile out of the Avenger. Dad grumpily sucking on his pipe, Mum wielding her sunken Victoria sandwich like a weapon and me, all long white knees socks and beige jumper. The one Elsie had knitted as last year's Christmas present.

"It would be rude not to wear it," Mum had stated, as we'd endured our usual sartorial stand-off in my bedroom.

I look about 50 I think gloomily, catching sight of my reflection in the car window. I sense movement in the front room even before we touch the knocker. Elsie and Blue Boy are keeping their eyes open for us. We march into the hallway in single file, our heads bowed.

Mum pushes me hard right in the direction of the front room. Reluctantly I go in. I smell lavender and camphor. Doilies adorn every surface. Waiting in the window is Blue Boy. His cage has pride of place. The budgie watches me with its blank shiny button eyes, all beady and spiteful. A bit like Aunty Elsie really.

"Blue Boy likes you." Elsie croons lovingly and with a total disregard for the truth.

The flea infested bird hates me I am certain. It's

viciously pecked me several times when I've attempted to feed it, as per Aunty Elsie's instructions.

Mum brings in the second best china service for us to eat off along with her collapsed cake.

Elsie eyes it. "See you've still not learnt the knack of getting them to rise?"

Mum smiles wanly. She long ago retired from any verbal battles with my Dad's aunty. Historically she's always lost.

Elsie pokes her long bony index finger through the cage bars to tickle Blue Boy's breast feathers. The horrid bird lets her. I shudder at the thought of any such contact and sit on my hands.

Now to my total embarrassment, Elsie starts singing to him. Blue Boy perches with his head on one side, gazing at her. He looks like a broken marionette, I realise. I'm suddenly reminded of the puppet show I'd gone to with Mum.

Dad breezes in, "How did it go at the bingo then, Elsie?"

He's all fake jovial. This is his social face. It's painful to watch. "Win a fortune did you?"

Elsie smiles, but fails to look warmer. "That's for me and Blue Boy to know, Derek. It's my money and my business."

Dad falls silent. I turn to gaze out past the sticky lace curtains to the road where I begin to count the number of blue/black/red cars driving by in the next fifteen minutes. I watch the grey day turn wetter and more ashen. I tune out the adult chit chat as best as I can.

Years later, when I'm at Uni. Elsie died. In her will she bequeathed us Blue Boy's bird cage because 'she knew how much we'd loved him'.

About the author

Alyson lives in West Yorkshire with her husband, teen son and four rescue animals. Her short stories have appeared in print in the *Women in Horror Annual 2*, *Stories from Stone*, *DeadCades: The Infernal Decimation*, *Coffin Bell Journal 1*, *Crackers* and in three *Trembling with Fear* anthologies published by the Horror Tree. Her debut flash fiction collection, *Badlands*, was published in January 2018 by indie publisher, Chapel Town Books. Her supernatural story *Night of the Rider* is available as an e-book in the *Short Sharp Shocks Series* from Demain Publishing. The *Ladies in Horror Fiction* blog narrated one of her stories on their pod-cast recently and her dark fiction appears regularly in the *Siren's Call* ezines. Alyson is a regular on the open mic circuit in Yorkshire too.

Her blog can be found at www.alysonfayewordpress.wordpress.com.

Her amazon author is at https://www.amazon.co.uk/l/B01NBYSLRT and she's on twitter as @AlysonFaye2.

Dignity and Injustice
Allison Symes

Black coffee

I was there when she died, you know. That is one advantage to being a time travelling alien. I can pretty much go to any era and explore it from the inside. Okay I have to disguise myself well but I can do that easily enough. Looking like a Tudor peasant is simple and, having befriended her daughter, I had to see for myself.

Elizabeth doesn't know what I am. There is no way to explain but she does know I am her friend and, like her, remained single, despite all the pressures to do otherwise. In my case, I fled my world to get away from my intended. He might have intended. I had no official say in the matter but decided the one who knew what was best for me was me. Elizabeth is very like that.

So here I am at the Tower of London on 19th May 1536. It will be a date that goes down in history. And why am I here at a prime spot near the scaffold? It's not morbid curiosity to see how Anne Boleyn died. It's a wish to know what to say to Elizabeth. She barely mentions her mother but often looks at the locket with Anne's portrait in it and is doing so more since the Scottish Queen's death. I want to tell Elizabeth I am sure her mother faced her unjust death with dignity but I can't lie. That does seem to be a human trait. I've got to know.

I must say, as I watch Anne being led out, she is graceful and calm. Two qualities that monster she married has never had. I am touched by her speech.

And then it is over. I find tears in my eyes and look up to see many here, who disliked, even hated, Anne in life also tearful.

But in a way I am content. I can return to Elizabeth and speak true when she is ready to talk about her mother. I can speak with conviction I am sure Anne met her end bravely. I just pray it will be enough.

About the author
Allison Symes writes fairytales with bite as flash fiction, novels and short stories. Her flash fiction collection, *From Light to Dark and Back Again*, was published by Chapeltown Books in 2017. She is a member of the Association of Christian Writers and Society of Authors. She adores P.G.Wodehouse, Jane Austen and Terry Pratchett. Allison's main website is www.fairytaleswithbite.weebly.com and she blogs for *Chandler's Ford Today* at http://chandlersfordtoday.co.uk/author/allison-symes/

The Lady in Red

Caroline S Kent

Black coffee

The rain hammered down hard, bouncing off the tarmac as hit it the ground.

Sitting in the National Express Mag Lev shelter outside of the main building the British serviceman was protected from the worst of the elements, but he was still damp and feeling miserable. He didn't feel like talking to his fellow travellers which is why he now sat outside in the open fronted shelter, his kit bag propped up in the corner behind him.

He was returning from his last posting in Nairobi for six weeks of accumulated leave, and he had looked forward to seeing his girlfriend when just two days before he had received the dreaded "Dear John" email which is why he was now pondering what to do.

Now with no one to look forward to spending time with and with no parents to visit, for he was an orphan, he had no specific place to go. He had zero intention of visiting the orphanage as he had no good memories of the place. In fact it was the main reason he was a soldier. As soon as he could pass for old enough he had run away to join up to escape the place. He had been underage back then but he was tall and well built; so with falsified papers he had managed to bluff it and join up.

Nursing a cold cup of bland vending machine coffee he pondered on if he should go back at all, or if he should go somewhere else entirely different and have a good time whoring, or gambling, both perhaps?

Another National Express Mag Lev pulled up to the other side of the station and was headed somewhere else. Looking at the Mag Lev's destination board he read that it was bound for Edinburgh. Perhaps Edinburgh wasn't such a bad idea he wondered.

As he was considering changing his ticket to Edinburgh instead a bolt of lightning lit up the night sky.

Well if I ever needed a sign from a God, he thought. With that he got up and started to stride towards the main station.

As he approached the stations main terminal he saw *her* stepping off the National Express Mag Lev. He didn't know her name or anything about her, but he knew, just knew that it was *her*, the one he had been looking for all of his life. She turned and looked straight into his eyes as her foot touched the ground.

Her tawny, gold-flecked eyes glancing towards him told him everything that he needed to know, like a proverbial thunderbolt from the sky mimicking the very real one just a moment before. Her knee length flowing crimson red dress made her stand out even more in this dreary, rain sodden day. She wore no coat or protection from the elements, yet she stood proud and untouched by the cold and rain. Like an Amazonian princess standing proud before her army.

His feet picked up a pace on their own and in no time at all he was running towards her, but she was still over fifty yards away. She turned away from him and then walked around the corner of the building and out of his sight. He faltered in his steps. He knew, just knew that she was the one for him and that he had seen the same recognition in her eyes. So how could she now turn away from him and walk away?

He felt fate pull him along as his feet started again all by themselves and he was running again towards her. He turned at the corner of the station and what he saw caused his heart to skip a beat: an empty yard! The large pale red brick-walled yard was just a parking lot for the Mag Levs and he could see no exit. Neither could he see her. She had been out of his sight for just a few seconds. So how had she just disappeared?

He quickly ran over the last few moments in his mind wondering if he had imagined it all. But no, there was a crushed cup in his right hand, no longer containing any coffee, having spilled out in his fifty yard sprint. He looked all around the empty yard in hope that he had missed a doorway, something, anything, to give a sign where the tall raven haired, tawny-eyed woman had disappeared to. There was: nothing. She was gone, vanished into thin air.

He turned to walk back when a glint caught the corner of his eye. He spun round, but there was nothing there. Thinking that this was getting stranger by the second he resolved to walk every inch of the yard, check every corner, every brick to see if he could have missed any escape route for the striking beauty that he had chased after.

A little over ten minutes later he was still none the wiser. As he shivered, realisation dawned on him that it was still raining and that he was now drenched through. Looking at his watch the time was 19:05 and his Mag Lev to Newcastle was due in ten minutes.

But should he go to Edinburgh instead?

About the author
Caroline S. Kent a lady of distinction who likes wine, women and chocolate, probably in that order.

The Untrodden Snow
Paula R C Readman

Stale wine

"Please, Megan I need more time." I shouted down the phone even though I'd promised myself I wouldn't.

"Mum, we've already talked this over. I need to get my life back on track. It's a great opportunity for me. One, I'm sure, Dad would've wanted me to take. I need you to be pleased for me."

"I am. Of course, I am," I lied.

"It's been five years, Mum. We agreed that I would help run the business until you were back on your feet again, but if an opportunity arose then I had to take it."

"I know, but I thought you would've waited until I'm…" I paused, not trusting myself.

Five years ago, my world fell apart when Laurence left. No, not just my world, but Megan's too. I couldn't really expect her to put her life on hold forever. It's supposed to get easier, but it doesn't. All it does is turn you into a hard-headed dragon that roars selfishly at everyone around you.

I wanted Megan at home because she reminded me so much of her father, not just her looks, but her strength too. Oh, she's right. I needed to regain my independence, but America. It's too far away.

"Look Mum," she said, her voice cracking. "Once I've found a place of my own, you'll be able to join me."

I knew she didn't want to upset me, but I couldn't stop the feeling that she was deserting me too. I wanted to say I'm stronger now, but I didn't feel it in my heart.

I heard her exhale, and felt her trepidation, but I held back not wanting the selfish dragon to scream down the line, "it's all right for you, but *what about me?*"

"Mum, think about it. A change of scenery will do you good." Her voice lightened. "You can come and stay for as long as you want. When the time is right, maybe you could sell up and join me here. Anyway, at least think about it. I know it's been hard on you, but Dad would've wanted you to enjoy your life. Please remember Mum, I miss him too."

"I know, Love."

Her voice softened. "Mum, you really need to start thinking about yourself. You're still young."

"Old head on young shoulders," I muttered.

"What? What did you say, Mum, I couldn't hear you?"

"Nothing darling," I said brightly, not wishing her to feel guilty about leaving.

"Mum, they're calling my plane. I've got to go now."

"Promise, you'll call me as soon as you touch

down." I said mustering a cheerful voice, wanting to give her something positive.

"Of course I will. I love you, Mum."

Normally the 'Rambler's Rest' would've been fully booked in the winter, just as it was in the summer months, but I wanted Christmas alone, so I allowed the bookings to dwindle. It surprised Laurence and me just how many people wanted to escape Christmas, so they booked a holiday away from it all.

For the first time I understood their need to be on their own. I hoped the time I spent alone would allow me to start planning a new future. As I stood by the French windows, at the back of the property, wine glass in hand, staring at the vast, empty moorland, I found myself watching the first snowfall of the season. As the imperfections of the world disappeared under a white quilt, the snowflakes became a flood blocking out even the pale light of the full moon.

I found comfort in knowing that no two flakes were alike. Their uniqueness mirrored my own situation. I wondered if Laurence was still out there. Was he watching the snowflakes falling too? Had it really been five years since our last hurried goodbye and his promised return?

"Time changes everything," I muttered, drawing the curtains, shutting out the coldness before crossing to the fireplace, and adding another log to the dying embers.

As the fire erupted back into life, the log spat a spray of red and yellow sparks into the dimly lit room, reminding me that another Christmas had passed with no words from him. I poured another drink, and stretched out on the sofa, offering up a toast to my past.

Megan was right; I couldn't expect her to stay forever.

I sipped the wine, not really tasting it and watched the small dancing flames reinventing themselves, flaring up and then dying back. I tried recalling the sound of Laurence's voice, the touch of his lips and warmth of his embrace.

With a sudden shudder, I woke. The early morning sun leaked through a gap in the curtains, revealing the neglect that surrounded me. Among the detritus of discarded rubbish, dirty plates, and cold cups of tea that littered the dusty surfaces, my eyes settled on the collection of Christmas cards. They reminded me how much love there was still in my life.

I ran my tongue around my mouth trying to free it from the stale taste of the wine before I sat up. Aware for the first time, I was still on the sofa. I rubbed my forehead and tried to remember the last time I had given the place a damn good clean.

A little unsteady, I stood, and kicked the empty wine bottle away. It rolled under the sofa as if it too was ashamed of what it had done. I staggered to the bathroom and splashed cold water onto my face. As I patted it dry with a musty smelling towel, I looked up.

The mirror above the sink revealed another unwelcome friend. She stared back at me with questioning grey eyes.

"I know," I answered her. "I'll take a shower."

Stripping off, I stepped under the shower. The force of hot water took me back to the long hot summer when Laurence and I first met.

I'd just turned sixteen and was on my first holiday without my parents. Tall, lanky, and unsure of myself, I stayed with my widowed Aunt Iris. She belonged to a ramblers club.

One day as we waited outside a pub on the moors for the rest of the group to arrive, a tall, suntanned lad with fair hair and the brightest sky-blue eyes I had ever seen, joined us. As Laurence's parents and my Aunt chatted together, he strode happily along beside me.

During that time, I learnt how passionate Laurence was about the untamed moors and the natural world around us.

"Oh Sally, this landscape is so beautiful," he said as we followed the footpath ahead of the others. He would point out things of interest to me, from butterflies to flowers, stone circles, to circling buzzards. Soon I realised I had a rival for his love, but I understood why he loved her so.

I couldn't compete with her wild beauty, but I acknowledged his passion. She wasn't a selfish lover, sharing a deep sense of freedom with all who travelled her many footpaths and bridleways under a clear blue sky where the only sound heard was that of a skylark descending, with nothing around for miles, but a sea of grasses, heathers, gorse, and of course the sheep.

"Never be deceived by her gentle beauty," Laurence warned me as we wandered along hand in hand. "There's many hidden dangers among her dips and hollows."

After stepping out of the shower, I rubbed my hair dry and smirked into the mirror asking, "Why must all good things come to an end?"

It would've been far easier if he'd fallen sick and died, or even divorced me, but the sense of loss I suffered is too hard to bear. Death is final. There are no ifs or buts. And, divorce, at least you can shout at them. With Laurence's disappearance, there's no body, no one to shout at, just many unanswered questions.

For years, Laurence and I had promised ourselves a winter holiday at the 'Rambler's Rest' in Yorkshire, where our love first began. On Christmas morning, Laurence teased me awake.

"Are you awake, Sally?" he whispered, running his fingertips down my chin, neck and between my breasts.

"Please, Laurence," I mumbled sleepily, "allow me time to wake up first, my darling."

He kissed my lips, parting them with his tongue.

"Not that, my sweet, as nice as it is." He laughed and kissed me again. "Let's go for an early morning walk."

We wrapped up warm against the bitter, cutting winds and headed out. Our footsteps the first to break the virginal snow as we set off as soon as it was light enough to see. By midday, we headed back. The wind had dropped and the sun, though cold, was bright.

As we removed our boots in the utility room, Mrs Williamson popped her head round the door. "When you're ready, please will you join me in my private dining room for Christmas dinner?"

"Of course, we'd love too." After showering, Laurence and I got dressed up for the occasion. As I dried my hair, my husband commented on the falling snow.

"We got back just in time," he said as the snow obscured our footprints.

"Thank you for allowing us to join you," I said as Annie showed us to our seats.

"It's my pleasure. So nice to share my last Christmas here with you both, especially as I've known you two for such a long time," she chuckled.

"Your last Christmas?" Laurence said, his fork hovering in mid-air.

"Yes, since my husband passed away, my son suggested now would be a good time to put 'Rambler's Rest' up for sale. The time has come for me to do something else. Travel maybe."

Laurence's face lit up, and I knew what he was thinking.

"I'm sure it's a lot of hard work on your own.' he said, putting down his fork."

"Oh it's been worth it. I've enjoyed every day and will miss waking up to the wonderful views, and of course all my lovely guests. I hope whoever buys it enjoys the same life I've had living here."

No sooner than we had climbed into bed that night, Laurence hugged me tightly. "I've been thinking, Sally, isn't it about time we followed our hearts and…"

I placed a finger on his lips. "I knew it… you want to take over 'Rambler's Rest'?"

He nodded, and kissed my fingertips. "Downsizing and escape city living will do us both the world of good and our daughter too."

Before Annie handed over the keys to us, she explained, "Being so isolated here, anyone caught out in bad weather finds out quickly it's an unforgiving place. Be prepared for every occasion. Keep plenty of stores in as you can be cut off for months."

'Rambler's Rest' became a real family affair and a Mecca too for the dedicated walkers, who stay every year. During the summer months, some of Megan's university friends helped us out to earn extra pocket money.

After a few mild winters, Annie's warnings seemed unfounded until one bitter cold morning five years ago. If anyone had warned me what would've happened that day, I wouldn't have believed it.

By late afternoon, it had warmed slightly. Busy in the kitchen sorting out evening meals for our guests, I had the radio on, checking the weather forecast.

"The weather's on the turn. The sky's full of it," Laurence said, coming in with a bucket of coal and an arm full of logs. His blue eyes shone bright as his cheeks and nose from the cold outside. "Hmm, it smells lovely in here. You're making me feel hungry."

"Have the Highsmiths returned yet?" I asked, peering through the serving hatch into the dining room.

"I haven't seen them. The Roberts are in the lounge reading, and the Longmans went to get ready for dinner." Laurence said as he added some coal and another log to the range before emptying the rest of the coal into the box beside the burner.

"I'm worried about the Highsmiths." I checked on the turkey.

"I'm sure they'll be back soon." He looked out the window, at the gathering storm clouds crossing the pale grey horizon.

"I just hope so. Anyone can see there's bad weather on the way."

He gave me a peck on the cheek. "Stop worrying. The smell of your food will have them rushing back,"

I began loading the dishwasher. "They arrived with no all-weathers-gear and went out this morning wearing designer trainers. Being Londoners, they might think it's like a stroll in Hyde Park on a winter's day."

"I'll go and have a word with the others. They might have seen them. Hopefully they're keeping to the main paths."

Laurence returned just as I was emptying the dishwasher, his face ashen.

"What is it, love?"

"The Roberts said they had seen them up by the old alum works."

"No, what were they doing up there."

"The Roberts told them to start heading back, but they wanted to finish exploring the works. What a pair of idiots!" Laurence snapped. "I'd best go and see if I can find them. To make matters worse it's snowing now, Sally."

"Laurence, you can't go on your own. It's a good hour's walk from here." I followed him through to the utility room.

"Hopefully, they're heading back. Call the rescue team, and warn them. Let's hope we don't need them." He pulled on his hiking boots, waterproofs, and an insulated jacket before grabbing a survival backpack. On opening the back door, a blast of cold wind hit us. "I'll be back before you know it," he said and disappeared out into the swirling snowflakes.

With no last goodbye kiss, not even an 'I love you.' Laurence rushed off to look for the Highsmiths. I forced the door shut behind him, and hurried to make the call.

"Roger, it's Sally from Rambler's Rest. Laurence has gone to the old alum works to see if he can find two of our missing guests. Yes, he knows the weather is closing in, but he didn't want to leave them out there. Be careful Roger, I'll see you soon."

After feeding the rest of guests and supplying hot drinks to some of the rescue party who arrived back tired, cold and unsuccessful in their search, I stood, by the window, hot chocolate in hand, as night drew in.

Through the snow flurries, I saw a group of figures, little more than crude outlines, their heads down, battling against the wind, which was trying to erase them. Once they crossed the threshold, I searched among the familiar faces unable to find Laurence.

The Highsmiths huddled together by a roaring fire, holding mugs of hot chocolate while through chattering teeth they thanked everyone for finding them. The rescuers stood round despondently, waiting for the storm to break so they could look for Laurence. After a week of searching, they finally had to call it off.

After thanking them all, I went onto the snow driven moors and screamed out his name, begging for his return.

With Megan's help, I focused on the business setting our loss to one side. With a bright smile, I sent my guests off hiking for the day, though secretly, I hoped that one of them would stumble upon Laurence's backpack, mobile, or even a boot. Anything that would let us know what had become of him, but of course, they were here to enjoy their holidays, not to free me from my sadness.

The first winter without Laurence left me feeling like Catherine Earnshaw as I longed for the return of my Heathcliff. Sometimes, when I was preoccupied with cleaning, a flash of brilliant light would illuminate the room. Dashing to the window, I was sure I could see his familiar form striding across the flat, valley floor towards the stile that marked our boundary.

As he clambered over, he would give me a wave, his signal to have his glass of brandy ready by the roaring fire in the lounge to take the chill from his bones.

Now dressed, I jammed the wet towels in the washing machine, and noticed the calendar. Three months had passed since Megan went to America. She's right about a change of scenery, though I'm not sure whether America is what I need right now.

Outside, I hugged my coat to me. The sharp, cold air, takes my breath away as I stroll towards the stile. A sudden "*kiew*" makes me look up. Overhead a buzzard circles, soaring high against the white sky before disappearing from view.

"Oh Laurence, my darling." I let my tears fall, knowing the time has come.

"*Kiew, Kiew,*" echoes across the icy landscape, pulling me out of my thoughts. Above the buzzard had returned, and with it, its mate.

As they circled, I acknowledged them, knowing that the moorland mistress has won. I whispered, "He's yours to keep."

I climb back over the stile, and see the signs of rebirth in the melting snow as blades of dull green with the drooping heads of snowdrops nodding gently in the cold breeze. They are the ones Laurence and I planted during our first spring here so long ago.

Maybe it was just my imagination, though I like to think its Laurence's way of letting me know it is time for me to move on.

He may be lost to me, taken by the mistress of the moor, who has his heart, body and soul. Wherever Laurence's final resting place is, he is not alone, with the buzzards, curlews, and the standing stones.

I hurry back to the warmth of the 'Rambler's Rest'. Tomorrow, I shall wish Megan a happy New Year, and ask if she's ready for a visit from her Mum.

Like snowflakes falling, I'll take things one step at a time, and who knows where the future may lead me.

About the author
Paula R C Readman left school at 16 with no qualifications and worked in low paying jobs. In 1998, she decided to beat her dyslexia by setting herself a challenge to become a published author. She taught herself 'How to Write' from books which her husband purchased from eBay. After 250 purchases, he finally told her 'just to get on with the writing'. Since 2010 she had 24 stories published, won three competitions, and is now busy trying to find a publisher for her first novel.

Blog: http://paulareadman1.wordpress.com

A Walk in the Woods

Jo Dearden

Damson wine

Crisp sun, clear skies. Leaves crunching underfoot.
A myriad of oranges, reds and yellows. A bright
autumn day. That was then. Now, the leaves seem
muted and the sky is leaden with a dreary greyness.
Trees are being stripped, their bareness a painful
reality like mine. I am no longer wanted.

We are walking in the woods above Acorn Hill.
Thick bracken clings to my muddy boots making me
stumble. Brambles entangle themselves in my hair
and graze my coat as I blindly follow Nick. Fallen
twigs crackle, disturbing the suffocating silence that
has descended upon us like a thick fog.

Nick is slightly ahead of me, shoulders hunched,
hands thrust into his pockets. He looks as though he
would rather be anywhere else than here with me. I
had no idea that anything was wrong. I suppose I
should have seen it coming, but love is blind. I still
love him. I think I always will. I can feel the rain
falling softly on to my tear-stained face as we walk
like strangers through the shadowy woods.

Dusk is rapidly approaching. A cold wind rustles
the remaining leaves on the half-naked trees.
Branches above my head have formed a hostile
canopy. The rain is more persistent, echoing our

escalating misery. My boots sink deeper into the mud. Nick trudges on ahead of me. He seems to be oblivious of the pervading gloom.

"I think we should go back now before it gets dark," I call feebly, but he doesn't seem to hear me. After a few moments he turns around and walks towards me.

"Look Jen, I'm really sorry. I'm not sure what I want yet. I just need some space." His words pierce like a sword into my soul. Nick and I have loved each other for what seems forever. We met at Edinburgh University, both reading English. We clicked from the start and it wasn't long before we were living together. Our friends said we were made for each other. Anna said she expected to be a bridesmaid. But now the dream is over, dashed to pieces by a few painful words.

The woods appear much darker than before. The twilight envelops us like a shroud. A twig snaps loudly making me jump. It is only a rabbit, but in the gloom my imagination is running riot.

"You're right, we'd better get back. I really want us to stay friends," Nick says. We both know that will be impossible, too painful after all we've been through together. It is raining heavily now. Dead leaves swirl at my feet. Everything seems dead. My new jeans are spattered with mud. I feel cold and tired.

We emerge from the oppressive woods into a

large open field. The hills on the horizon merge with the colourless sky. Below is a tiny hamlet. Smoke is curling from some of the cottage chimneys. We stop for a moment catching our breath.

"We'll be ok Jen," Nick says squeezing my hand. A last ray of sun appears in the watery sky.

About the author

Jo Dearden trained as a journalist with the Oxford Mail and Times. She did a degree in English Literature with Creative Writing as a mature student. She co-edited her local village newsletter for about ten years. She also worked for a number of years for the Citizens' Advice Bureau. She is currently attending a creative writing class, which is stimulating her writing again. Jo lives in Suffolk.

Father Van Der Bosch's Last Christmas
Robin Wrigley

Mulled wine

It was the last Friday, a week before Christmas, and Jens Van der Bosch was walking through the alley from his residence in the walled city of Jerusalem. He had been invited for dinner by an old acquaintance, Maurice the manager of the Sinai Hotel, outside the old city walls.

Dusk was approaching. Various craft and workshop vendors were either closing down their shutters for the night or busy rearranging their wares and checking the lighting. Though he knew most of them by sight, and in some cases by name, he endeavoured not to offer any greetings in order to avoid the inevitable time consuming cups of tea that would lead to his being late for his appointment.

As he silently walked through the labyrinth, turning this way and that, his feet knew the directions so well having trod this way so many times over the years; he was able to allow his thoughts into reflections rather than needing to concentrate on the route.

He had taken up this post as a novice, forty-one years ago at the age of twenty-three; now he was nearing retirement in this year on his sixty-fifth birthday. All too soon he would be a resident at the Franciscan retirement hospice in his native Holland.

A slight chill came over him at the mere thought of it.

Where had the years gone? He smiled to himself as he remembered his first month trying his utmost to blend in and learn the art of obsequiousness in order to fit in to the ways of this smouldering, melting pot of the three major religions without fear or favour.

Unexpectedly it had snowed the first week in January that first year, something he never ever considered likely. He thought he had left snow and ice behind in Europe. But snow it did and he fondly remembered the look of righteous indignation of the camel hunkered down outside one of the tourist hotels; a white blanket slowly forming on his head and hump. How silly and incongruous he looked.

So much had happened in the intervening years – some good but mostly sad. That first year there had been much celebrating at the rescue of hostages in Entebbe. This was but the first of many significant events during his tenure and a classic example of the tenacity of this tiny nation to survive against overwhelming odds.

As he turned a sharp right out of the last alley that led to the main road to meet the hotel taxi, he almost collided with a young Rabbi hurrying for the start of the Shabbat.

The Rabbi almost lost his hat and Jens offered his profuse apologies in English. Though he had mastered Hebrew as well as Arabic he still was not comfortable in the former.

"My sincere apologies Rabbi, I'm afraid I was lost in thought. May I offer you the season's greetings? Merry Christmas."

The Rabbi glared back, righted his black Homberg hat and attempted to continue on his way but not before spitting loudly on the cobbles. Jens was extremely upset at such a response but in forty plus years he had learned a lot and not all from his calling or the bible. He had the advantage of middle-age; the Rabbi was but a young man and given to such outbursts.

He turned around embracing the Rabbi quietly but firmly and kissed him on each cheek. The Rabbi recoiled and pushed him away – he had spent over an hour ceremoniously dressing and preparing for the lighting of the candles. Now this stupid priest had defiled him and he would have to return to his home and begin the ritual all over again.

Father Jens Van der Bosch continued on his way out onto the main street to the waiting taxi. Having greeted the driver with all the necessary politeness he settled into the back seat with a smile on his face. A life of many twists and turns and the year was coming to its natural conclusion. But first he was to have supper with Maurice.

About the author
Robin, a relative newcomer to short story writing, has spent the majority of his adult life as a land surveyor and later a country manager working in over twenty countries

world-wide. The variety of the situations he has faced and the people he has met inspired him to create many of his stories. His stories have been featured both on line and in print with CaféLit as well as two other short story collections. He is a member of the Wimborne Writers' Group.

Gemini Rising

Paula R C Readman

Leaping Legend (Badger Beers)

I felt no warmth as I lay huddled under my trench coat against the bitter cold wind, wanting nothing more than to return home. The weather seemed on change as the strength of the wind grew enough to sweep the clouds away.

I turned my aching head towards the heavens. The night sky revealed its magnificence to me in a multitude of stars that I could almost reach out and touch.

Though I had my sleeping comrades-in-arms close by, I felt alone. I scanned the array of galaxies, focusing on the constellations, hunting for the twins, Pollux and Caster. On finding them together for all eternity, a tear slipped down my cheek as thoughts of my brother Osbert, older by two minutes, filled my mind. On seeing Gemini rising, I longed to be back at his side in the landscape of our birth where we drew our first breath together.

As the night wore on, I grew as restless as the wind with its constant complaining. It shook and rattled everything in its path as it raced across the land. I closed my eyes, finding it hard not to inhale the stench of death. I wondered what the wind had to complain about when it had such freedom to go wherever it pleased.

When the time came for my leaving, it was as unexpected as my arrival. Exhausted by the battle in a foreign land that was not mine, I was glad to be going home, and travelled by whatever means was available to me as I made my way across Europe.

I was relieved to be back on English soil, though I knew my journey was only just beginning. I took the first available train heading out of London, and found myself in the compartment with a white-haired old gentleman, dressed in tweeds, who sat nodding asleep. Careful not to disturb him, I took the window seat.

Weary, not just from the journey I had made, but worn out from the fear of facing my father after his reaction to my leaving. As strange as it may seem to others after the terrors I had faced when I heard the sounds of dying men's screams in the name of freedom, I should fear facing my father far more.

I closed my eyes briefly, rested my head against the cold glass. The rattling of the train as it gathered speed made me recall the angry words my father and I had exchanged.

"Then go, my son, fight your battle in the Balkans if you must, but remember; whom the gods love dies young."

With that, he turned and walked away. I couldn't

understand why he was against my going. We were young men who were about to stand and fight for freedom.

In the end, he would not listen to me, or I to my brother's pleas. To prove them all wrong, I followed my friends into hell.

As the train raced towards my destination, I watched the city fade from view until tiredness washed over me. On closing my eyes, I found myself back among the horrors, as the sounds of my friends' laughter became the screams of reality as one by one they lost their lives.

Suddenly, drawn away from my nightmare, I woke to find someone tapping on my shoulder. The gentleman seated opposite was using his walking stick to get my attention. I wiped my mouth on the back of my hand, and apologised for my dreams disturbing his peace.

His soft sympathetic brown eyes held mine as he shook his head, "Fear not lad, it's I who disturbs you, but only to let you know we've reached your destination."

I straightened up and said, "Sorry, but… how did you know?"

He smiled kindly. "There's no mystery, young sir. I overheard you at the ticket office."

I shook my head, a little puzzled. I tried to recall buying a ticket, but found only a blur of half-evoked thoughts and feelings in my exhausted mind. I dismissed it concerned only with my father's reaction on seeing my return.

My journey home was quicker than I had expected. Instead of arriving early the next morning, it was late afternoon when I alighted at our rural station. I found it quite deserted apart from the old stationmaster, who I was sure had retired many years ago.

He seemed to study me for a moment, a stranger standing so forlorn on his platform. Then his face brightened, "Goodness me, is it really you, young Charles Ratcliffe. My, haven't you grown."

"War changes you, sir. A boy doesn't remain for long on a battlefield."

His watery eyes narrowed in bewilderment, "A battlefield?"

"Yes, the Balkan wars, sir."

With a slow nod, his eyes met mine. "Your father will be right pleased to have you home. It will spare him the not knowing what had become of you."

I smiled politely, "It may've spared him, but many others have been robbed of good men who have died for what they believed in."

He lowered his cap and said, "Too true, young sir." After a nervous hesitation, he asked, "I'm sorry there isn't anyone here to meet you. Were you expected today?"

I glanced at the station clock and was puzzled to see it had stopped at two o'clock.

"Are you all right, young Charles?"

I turned and smiled an apology, "Just a little weary, I guess. My return was unexpected, giving me no time to let them know."

He smiled kindly, "May I wish you God's speed as you make your final journey homeward."

I left the station on foot. After an hour, I paused to take in the view. Everything was exactly as I remembered it. Far below, a cluster of sandstone buildings gathered beside an old stone bridge. The fertile land deep within a valley had for generations been home to my ancestors who had lived and worked the lands all around.

"Your final journey homewards," I muttered, echoing the station master's words. Suddenly the sunlight caught the water's surface making it sparkle so brightly it dazzled me, blinding me briefly as the sound of rooks and crows filled the air.

Being the youngest of three sons neither the Jacobean hall, nor its land would be mine to inherit. Generations ago, things might have been different; my brothers may have fallen foul of childhood illnesses, a death on some distance battlefield or even an irate husband as befell some of my predecessors.

I wondered for a moment whether my family had

received my last letter, telling them that I was well after receiving their shocking news about the death of my oldest brother, Robert.

It had shocked me to the core. I couldn't have believed it was possible for him to die in such a peaceful and beautiful place? To add to my misery I'd been unable to return home to attend his funeral, yet days later I find myself travelling home.

As the cawing of the circling rooks and crows bring me out of my reverie I know, if I am to reach home before the sunset, I must make haste.

For too long I'd been away from the rich English soil and now all I wanted was to feel it under my fingernails instead of blood and burning flesh.

When my father inherited the Radcliffe estate from his indebted father after he had gambled the family fortune away, he made sure his sons knew every aspect of what it took to run such a large estate. I enjoyed my time working alongside the gardeners, gamekeepers, and farm managers. To me, coming home was so much more than just asking for my father's forgiveness. It was about returning to the place I wanted to be and to raise a family of my own.

On arriving at the front door, I was shocked to find a wreath of laurel pinned to it. The house seemed to be in darkness, though it was still too early for my family to take to their beds. I feared the worst as I reached for the door handle, but to my surprise, it swung open, and it was with a heavy heart, I entered.

The air within was heavily laden with the sweet, sickly smell of lilies. I stood for a moment puzzled by the silence. The huge grandfather clock of my childhood stood silent, yet it was something my father took pride in for its ability at keeping good time.

The only sound in the house I could hear was the black ribbons on the wreath as they fluttered in time with the wind in the trees outside. I heard no sound of my family or the servants.

Where was everyone?

Within the entrance hall, the only light available for me to see by came through the open door as I took in my surroundings. I explored further, and soon found the reason for the darkness; someone had closed shutters.

Beyond an ornate screen, I found on the refectory table an open empty coffin with two large silver candlesticks alight surrounded by flowers.

My puzzlement quickly left when I realised they must have received my last letter, and had delayed Robert's funeral until I had returned home.

On finding no one about, I went to my old familiar childhood bedroom, with its high ceiling and four-poster, and settled down to sleep, hoping that by the morning there would be a simple explanation to everything.

I was startled awake, by what, I knew not. I crossed to the window and lifted the heavy frame. Outside dark clouds raced across the horizon, adding to the sense of unease that crept over me. Threads of a vivid dream clung to me like wasps at a picnic.

In my dream, I saw my family waiting for my arrival, but instead of their smiling faces to welcome their prodigal son back home, they were dressed in their mourning clothes and in receipt of a flimsy coffin from an unfamiliar stationmaster and his guardsman. With frayed nerves, I picked up my lamp and went to search for my brother, Osbert.

I entered his bedroom, a mirror image of my own room. A lofty four-poster dominated the spacious room. Its faded tapestry canopy and curtains were now dusty with age.

Within my lamplight, the particles of dust danced as I moved across the room. My brother lay on his back; his china-blue eyes tightly shut in an unnatural deep sleep, his face, a replica of mine, with its strong nose, full mouth, and pale skin. Although I felt chilled, sweat dampened my brother's dark brown hair, plastering it to his fine forehead.

As I reached out to rouse him, his eyes sprung open. Something in the room shifted and I felt my brother's eyes focused on me briefly, halting me in my action. As Osbert's eyelids drooped, I felt time detached itself from me as a feeling of dislocation swept over me. I backed away from the bed, my heart lurched sickeningly, caught somewhere between fear and panic.

I descended the stairs in a rush. The lamp I held cast ghostly shadows across the sombre painted faces of my ancestors who stared blankly back at me as if to remind me just how fleeting time is for the living. In the hall, the sickly sweet perfume filled air seemed to choke the life out of me.

Drawn once again to the screen, I ran my fingertips over the family crest and felt an increase in my discomfort as I pushed open the gate to find someone had closed the coffin.

Shock filled my mind. Why hadn't the noise of their carriages returning so late woken me? Surely, the sound of them closing a heavy oak coffin in such an enclosed space would've been enough to wake the dead.

With a heavy heart, I rested my hand upon the smooth wood. All I wanted to do was to resolve the unhappiness I had caused between father, my two brothers, and myself. At least showing my last respects to Robert now may compensate some of my foolishness, in my father's eyes.

"Fear not Charles, you're not alone."

On hearing the sound of Osbert's voice, I turned, surprised that I hadn't heard him sooner.

"Osbert," I said, as he walked towards me, "I'm sorry I didn't mean to wake you." I stepped back and watched as he stood as I had done with his hands resting on the coffin as though to draw comfort from it.

Then he whispered, "I'm so sorry that our last words together were spoken in anguish."

"Oh, brother it's not you who should apologise, but I," I said smiling brightly; glad that we could speak openly, but I was puzzled that he didn't meet my gaze.

"I must be strong," he continued as though I wasn't there, "for Father needs me after losing another."

"Another?" I said, puzzled.

"Father blames himself for not being there, when the stake killed Robert outright after the wind had whipped the tarpaulin off the hayrick, and now to lose you," he sobbed.

"No, I'm here, look," I stepped towards him, wanting to shake him. Then I noticed a framed photograph draped in black velvet. Alongside it, the family bible lay open. I knew the marked verse off by heart.

It was our favourite; understanding the love, the brothers Saul and Jonathan felt *that not even death could divide them.*

I pulled the cover off the photograph, knowing it was true. Remembering how the stars faded from the sky that night my head had ached so much.

"Please accept our forgiveness, Charles. Death will not part us for long," Osbert sobbed, crossing to the stairs.

"Wait!" I called after him.

"Do not be afraid," a voice said. "Though your brother can't hear you, he senses you're here."

I turned to find the white-haired gentleman from the train standing at my side, "Who are you?"

"Fear not, I'm one of the guides sent to help restless spirits find their way home. Your time has come to leave now."

"So it wasn't a dream, when I saw my family gathered at the station?"

"No, it wasn't. Accept your brother's forgiveness; it will at last set you free, Charles."

I nodded, feeling the peace I had longed for filling my heart. As my spirit lifted, I knew I would soon be joining Robert and my other ancestors who'd gone before.

About the author

Paula R C Readman left school at 16 with no qualifications and worked in low paying jobs. In 1998, she decided to beat her dyslexia by setting herself a challenge to become a published author. She taught herself 'How to Write' from books which her husband purchased from eBay. After 250 purchases, he finally told her 'just to get on with the writing'. Since 2010 she had 24 stories published, won three competitions, and is now busy trying to find a publisher for her first novel.

Blog: http://paulareadman1.wordpress.com

The First Time
Robert Daley

Tea, no sugar

The first time you break up with someone, unexpected stuff can really throw you off.

I'd been unfaithful, more than once. The last time a week ago, with an escort. You know how it is, when you're twenty, you'd fuck a roll of tin foil if it landed in your lap. We'd lasted eighteen months.

"I don't see this going anywhere," I told her. But it wasn't so. She'd been through my wallet, left the cards out of order. Some women don't even need evidence.

"I see." She grinned as she scooped a spoonful of sugar from the bowl and gently lowered it into her tea.

I said, "You're taking it well." She was resilient, for sure, the type of woman who could give birth on her lunch break and work the afternoon shift. Even so, no tears?

"I've been seeing Jim." She gripped a red lock of hair like it was an alarm cord. Stirred her tea some, generating a surge of steam. Jim was a barman at the Kensington members' club where she waited tables. I'd met him once when I picked her up at the end of the night. He offered me a drink on the house, a glass of red. His smile could disarm an angry old lady of her cane.

"How long's *that* been going on?" I cracked my knuckles.

"Three weeks or so." She pressed her knees together. I knew it'd been longer. I could have thrown my tea in her face. But I drank it and poured another. I wanted sugar but she had the spoon. I couldn't bear asking for it.

About the author
Robert is a forty-five-year-old student mental health nurse, studying at the University of the West of England. He lived in Japan for ten years, and has recently been inspired by the works of Haruki Murakami. He now resides in Stroud, UK.

Bats Downunder

Mehreen Ahmed

Dessert wine

They sat by the lake.

Mila Chowdhury did. Papri's fiancé Rahim Rahman did. They waited for Papri. Rahim, wore rimless reading spectacles. He took them off and looked at Mila with the bare eye. Mila felt uncomfortable. She made no eye contact, but she knew that Rahim continued to look at her. Mila was distracted by a host of flying foxes headed for an unknown destination. They flew self-organised in perfect harmony. A vulture swooped low by the lake and picked up food scraps left overnight by people. Those who may have picnicked here by the lake. Or had nameless yearnings for transcendence under the midnight stars and shimmering moonlight.

Such yearnings burned at the far end of an alley too. This place, disreputable for scandalous affairs, juxtaposed crudely to Mila's, grandparent's respectable House of Chowdhury, situated within a short distance in the same neighbourhood. Known as the fallen zamindars, or kings of a principality, their old money shielded them from being pushed out in the cold. It was not a bleak house. In their own right, they basked in the glory of being one of the most influential families in all of East Pakistan, now

Bangladesh. Patrons of art and culture, they made sure that there was never any dearth of culture in this house. The members of the family paid visits to the local cinema theatres nearly every week, streaming the dashing, postmodern hero Waheed Murad's top hits.

Many neighbours thought this house was a fun house; endless joy emanated from here. Every evening, a huge straw mat carpeted its front yard amongst the monsoonal tiger lilies and thorny roses; a secret garden grew hidden in the foliage of juicy berries and tall neem trees. Short of an oriental paradise, the image of an idyllic moon conjured a midsummer night's dream, in which mad Puck's touch sparked many emotions of tenderness and romance to boot. The members of the House of Chowdhury jostled tonight on the mat to listen to their youngest son, Ashik sing. He sang love songs – songs that would easily melt the hearts of many.

He surely ignited romance in one such woman, the neighbour Raja Hashem's wife, Bibi Khadijah. Bibi in the language meant 'the wife'. Bibi Khadijah, the young mother of three, craved for Ashik's company beyond the legal limits of friendship. Her own husband, failed to amuse her. And this provoked an unsavoury behaviour in turn. She moved further away from her husband and fell into an abyss of ennui. Only her love for this spirited youngest son gave her the thrill to live. Bibi Khadijah was a woman of great beauty, an enchantress by a long shot in the neighbourhood. She didn't think that age mattered. Ashik was five years younger than her. He was only twenty-five and she, thirty.

When the House of Chowdhury woke up to Ashik's songs, Bibi Khadijah could not restrain herself. Regardless of the various moods exuded from those songs, melancholic or lively, she thought, he sang them only for her. His love songs touched every beat of her heart. The lyrics that *I loved you so much that only the moon knew its depths*. Whether or not, he sang them out of deference to her, or out of actual love, no one could tell. But as time rolled by, and time and time again, those very lyrics sung in her presence, were like a call of nemesis to her ears. They left her undone. Trying to stay confined in her own house was futile. Neither could she stop listening to the songs, which could be heard anyway, because of the close proximity between the two houses, separated by a flimsy gated wall. By any stretch of imagination, on a full moon, this garden reshaped into the mango grove in her mind, where the enchanted Krishna and his Gopis came down to play. To Bibi Khadijah, they seemed to perform ritual dances to the magical tunes. At behest of her muses, she felt like a Gopi herself to the amorous god, whose open invitation awaited to resume romancing.

Such unbridled thirst pulled her towards the house like a star to a black hole; it behooved her to respond to her senses. Songs, which made her feel beautiful. She felt whole in all those jewellery and the saris she wore. They made her forget about the chores and her children and the drudgery of a prosaic husband, Raja Hashem, who seemed to live in his own world anyway; like a happy idiot, oblivious to everything.

His name, Ashik, meant lover. Ashik couldn't deny that he too desired the young mother, Bibi Khadijah; the forbidden fruit, a mother of three, and married to the neighbour. They both knew that love neither understood, nor respected any boundaries. It was literally coveting the neighbour's wife. However, nothing could or ever would obliterate the feelings they harboured for each other. Nor keep them away from their mischievous dates. The rendezvous? What other place, but the shady end of the alley. Just as well, the alley offered lovers like them some kind of recognition, a panacea to the souls, which cured them from all kinds of afflictions inflicted by society. A place where clandestine relationships thrived. Some were romantic interlude, others more promising. It was yet to be discerned, exactly how Ashik and Bibi Khadijah's relationship transpired.

Nevertheless, another romance blossomed right here in this house as well. A veranda enveloped the House of Chowdhury, whose privacy sheltered the lovers. Mila, saw it come to fruition. The hay-day of their lives, when the leaves of the guava trees trembled at the slightest touch of a pecking bird; its whistles whipped the core of young hearts; the agony of restive days and listless evenings; the sallow lantern didn't quite reach the far side of the balcony. Where in this dim obscurity, another young couple sat in two cane chairs with their fingers braided into each other. This couple was not Ashik and Bibi Khadijah, but a different pair of lovers from the same House of Chowdhury.

Her name was Lutfun Azhar, and his was Sheri Chowdhury. Lutfun, had just turned eighteen and Sheri, twenty. Cousins from their father's side, they dated here at sunset every evening. They didn't have to go to the alley, for theirs was a more legitimate relationship. Other members of the family recognised this relationship in tacit support which encouraged them further. Mila sensed the subtle sweetness in the air. She heard their words describe the nuances of love in quiet adoration for each other, summing up to heavy sighs, and soft murmurs. They also saw that their niece Mila, watched them without a din, but they smiled at her curiosity. They were not remotely bitter, nor concerned. There was no place for such negativity in their hearts, which oozed with the ripened juices of love.

Memories were always precious. Their tell-tale hearts told magical stories. Impossibly intense love stories; stories of Romeo and Juliet, and Laila and Majnu, which only inspired optimism. None of these tales ever happened concurrently. Never in the exact same sequence, nor in the same place. But in completely separate moments in history. Still, they spoke of the same profound themes of love in the sacred hearts alluding to no profanity. Invaluable tales gathered like a relic in the repository of the mind. Nostalgia heavy with gripe, rekindled. Good and bad entwined.

Lutfun was a virtuous women, kind and pious. She loved people unconditionally and her guileless smiles said it all. Her smiles beguiled everyone. She possessed a natural selflessness like the perfect Hyperborean land. Such innate endowments became stronger with every passing season. These were some of the qualities that made Sheri Chowdhury fall in love with her. The gentle lady that she was bestowed her affections readily upon Sheri. When Mila eavesdropped on their conversations, they let her in on it. She stood there in the dark passageway and listened away to every story they told. She observed how they kissed, held hands and whispered nothings at soft twilights.

It all seemed like a fable to Mila. That this sort of kindness should prevail in pursuance of love. Utopia, at best, something so divine that even time didn't or wouldn't tarnish. These were exemplary instances. However, they also provided a rare glimpse into the natural order of things of what should be, but rarely is. Like the perfect sun or the moon, or precise forces of gravitational pull, such love could find itself a home in the celestial pantheon, but few and far between. Sheri could easily die for Lutfun, as did Romeo for his Juliet.

A cloud rumbled. Mila looked up at the sky and then at Rahim, who by now had put his glasses on. He looked out at the lake unmindfully to say, "I wonder what's keeping her?"

"Hmm, don't know. There's going to be a storm soon," she said. "What should we do?"

"I don't know. At any rate, I don't think we can sit here anymore," he said. "Why not come over to my place. I've got my car."

"Thanks, I can walk home. My house is not very far," she said.

Rahim looked at her tentatively. Mila knew, he wanted her in his car somehow. But she felt awkward. What were they going to talk about anyway? Money? Investments? Those things didn't interest her. She looked up at the layered clouds against the vibrant autumn colours meeting on the edge of a dull horizon. Rahim kept a close watch hoping that somehow she would change her mind. But Mila's passions lay elsewhere. She was the quintessential introvert, who pondered and observed the world around her. No one would understand, nor even care for her love of incessant rain fall. The thunder, and the swishes of the gusty winds were music to her ears. Losing herself in the mists and the opaque drizzles of a ponderous sky, in her nature.

Mila didn't respond. He got into his car and drove away in moderate rage. She didn't understand the reason for this rage. Why would someone remotely related to her get upset? Apart from the fact that Papri Khandaker was a close friend of hers, there were no other ties with Rahim that he should be upset. Mila's refusal to get into his car, and then to his place wouldn't be right without her friend being present here. Her role models, uncle Sheri and the virtuous aunty Lutfun, would not approve. However, Bibi Khadijah and uncle Ashik may have, she wouldn't know. At any rate, in both cases, love had to spring both ways that brought people closer. Not force, much less anger.

Bibi Khadijah and Ashik were just as passionate as lovers, as any other couple without a doubt. However, they would never be allowed to date in the house like Sheri and his girl-friend Lutfun. Despite the fact that Ashik was Sheri's brother, Ashik and Bibi Khadijah dated far down by the alley with all other shady couples with equally shifty commitments. At Ashik's beck and call, Bibi Khadijah came out at nights after putting her children to bed. When her husband sat with the boring evening newspaper, she snuck out courageously to meet her lover, over by the designated lover's den.

The lovers' den was a cave in a small mountain conveniently located out of sight. At night time, lovers enshrined the cave with glowing candles. This was the moment when the cave became a sanctuary, illuminated with impassioned dialogues. This wasn't the place for Sheri and Lutfun at all, but only for the strays of the moor. Ashik Chowdhury wasn't one. He belonged to the same House of Chowdhury, a house held in high esteem. This dungeon was not the most sought after place for a lover like him. But his circumstance decreed otherwise. His amounted to an unsightly affair, a profanity, not seen in the same light of reverence as Lutfun-Sheri.

What difference did it make anyway, Mila thought in circumspect. Why should society condemn the types of the Lady Chatterley or the Madam Bovary? Were they any different from the Laila-Majnu, and the Romeo-Juliet kind as far as love was concerned? All's fair in love and war, wasn't it?

It depended on how those songs that Ashik sang on evenings really affected the people in the house. Surely, for Lutfun and Sheri, they meant love and worship of utmost purity. A union of a celestial pair sanctioned by society, favoured by their elders. Every other evening, they sat beside one another on the same mat under the watchful eyes of their elders, holding hands in perfect bliss, exchanging tiny, coy smiles. Whereas Bibi Khadijah would push herself in through the gate and hover at the fence darkly, like a dithering shadow, waiting for a welcome cry from someone to join the party on the mat. Although she and Ashik were Cupid blind as anyone else in love, the elders of the House of Chowdhury looked upon her as nothing other than the beautiful, lush wife of their quiet neighbour. Clueless to their affair, however, this the family would never have condoned, if they knew so much as a word.

Her husband Raja Hashem hardly spoke to anyone, but commanded huge respect in the neighbourhood on account of it. A learned man, Raja Hashem couldn't understand his wife's fantasies. To him three healthy meals, clothes, and ornaments sufficed; from head to toe, Bibi Khadijah was covered in jewellery like a Queen. But her insufferable ennui was hard to break. No one could. Not even her own children, apart from Ashik, could break the bounds of ennui. Although she couldn't go even remotely close to Ashik in the House of Chowdhury, she found a full life here in-spite of it, away from the stifling atmosphere of her own. For her husband wouldn't notice her great beauty, let alone compliment it. Deep in his studies, he lived a life of the mind, a scholar, until one day something knocked him.

One night, he decided to not to read his news-paper, but to engage with his wife. As he looked for her in the house, she appeared nowhere. He thought, maybe, Bibi Khadijah was with the neighbours, but he wished she were here tonight. As the night progressed, he gradually fell asleep. However, when he woke up in the morning, she was still not in bed. Her side of the bed had not been slept in all night. Suspicion didn't enter his mind, because he was not the sort. But when he entered the dining room for breakfast, he found his children sitting glumly without a mother. As soon as they saw their father, they broke down in tears.

Raja Hashem now feared the worst. He walked over to the veranda, and found a note pressed under the heavy volumes of *War and Peace* on a feeble cane table by the red rhododendrons. He saw it and swiftly pulled it out from under the two tomes. It read very clearly that Raja Hashem should not try to look for her as she had run away with her man next door. Was this some sort of a joke or serious elopement? Indeed, but as Raja Hashem struggled to grapple with the reality of the situation, he read the note a few times, and then looked at his children's innocent, sad expressions. They had no idea where their mother had gone, let alone, why she had gone. They stared wide-eyed at their befuddled father, who was at a loss for words himself. Then he grabbed his children in panic and embraced them with all his heaving heart.

It was bold, but no act of nobility. Raja Hashem's sanctimonious life, or at least how Bibi Khadijah would interpret it, did not keep her ennui at bay. What Ashik could give her, Raja Hashem could not. The couple settled at the far end of the alley, without the blessings of the House of Chowdhury. Their elopement did not make his family proud. It caused such turmoil, that Mrs. Chowdhury, the mistress of the house had to disown him. And Ashik, forced to part with the glory of the House of Chowdhury, thought this sacrifice justified his love for her. If Romeo-Juliet, Laila-Majnu could transcend to a metaphor for love, theirs could too one day. In the heart of it, he felt that they were equal. They had more in common, than naught. Because, in terms of the society's rebuke, none found a sympathetic hearing from any quarters. Conversely, Lutfun-Sheri thought of themselves as the proper embodiment of Romeo-Juliet, since they fared so well. But the definition of the real McCoy of the world remained indeterminate. Because, love machines like Lady Chatterleys always justified their affairs, not profane, but as just as sacred.

About the author:
Mehreen Ahmed is an internationally published and critically acclaimed author. Her books have been nominated for Aurealis Award for Fantasy Short Story/Novella (2015), Ditmar Awards for Best Novels (2016), and Author Academy Awards for Global Award Literary Merit and Publishing Excellence in Historical Fiction (2018). She lives in Australia.

Induction Day

Janet Howson

Charitea

She decided to dress in a comfortable fashion, if there was such a thing as a comfortable fashion, but she liked the word comfortable. It evoked childhood memories. "Are you sitting comfortably? Then we will begin." From that iconic children's radio programme. Or, "make yourself comfortable" her mother's final words before leaving the house to prevent unnecessary toilet stops. So comfortable was how she had dressed.

She chose a blue skirt; she had toyed with the idea of wearing trousers, she wasn't even sure what her role was going to be. They might decide to put her out the back of the shop (out of harm's way) sorting the mountainous black plastic bags overflowing with the general public's detritus. She hoped not. When she had seen the advertisement discreetly placed on the entrance door window "Volunteers required, please apply within" she had pictured herself smiling benevolently and welcoming customers as they entered the shop. Ringing up their purchases and asking them if they required a bag. Still time would tell.

She had decided on a white blouse that she often wore when she was working, paid work that is, not the voluntary type she was involved with now. She decided against the jacket she used to wear with the blue skirt, opting for a blue cardigan instead. When she retired she put all her suit jackets in a black bin liner and took them along to a charity shop similar to the one she would be volunteering at later. She knew she would never wear them again and they were only a painful reminder of past times.

Her earrings matched the blue outfit. She always felt naked without earrings. She used to say at work that she couldn't leave the house without her lipstick and earrings. She wasn't a vain person. Not like the young girls in the office who appeared to preen themselves most of the day talking in high pitched voices of the conquests they had made at the weekend. She knew they thought she was a dinosaur wearing what she wore but she didn't care what they thought. She kept herself to herself.

Shoes had proved to be a problem. She wasn't sure if boots would be appropriate or just sensible shoes. No teetering heels with thin straps, like the girls used to wear, but choosing flat brogues that would be kind to her bunions.

One last look in the mirror before she donned her coat. She called it her "duvet coat" as it was so thick and warm and had a fur-lined hood.

Oh, she nearly forgot. Her umbrella. She never went anywhere without her umbrella. Another legacy of her mother. The sky looked threatening, she might be glad of it later.

She had decided to walk. The shop shut at 4.30pm but she might be required to tidy up, sweep round or wash up the tea cups – she presumed there would be a cup of tea sometime during the afternoon? It would be far too long to leave her car in a car park. She objected to paying for a car park ticket. Once she had been three minutes late returning to pick up her car and was horrified to discover a yellow bag on the front windscreen announcing the parking penalty.

The walk normally took her twenty minutes into the centre of town. The charity shop was favourably placed being next to the main shops in the High Street. She had always made a beeline for a charity shop after doing the main stores first.

When she arrived at the shop a wave of nerves hit her. She almost turned back. However, she took a deep breath and entered. There were a few customers sorting through the hand rails and an elderly man standing behind the till, endeavouring with obvious difficulty to keep his eyes open. She assumed he was the morning shift. She also spotted a lady with her back to her sorting out the DVDs. She thought it would be wisest to approach the morning shift so donning a smile she approached the till.

"Hello, I am here for my Induction Day. I was told George Forbes would be going through everything with me. Do you know where I could find him?"

The man at the till was now wide-awake eyeing her suspiciously. After a moment he seemed to get a grip of the situation. "Wait here…" He was about to leave his sentry post by the till when something made him stop. "Can't leave the shop floor. Things get nicked. You'd be surprised how much stuff gets nicked. You wouldn't think people would be so callous as to steal from a charity shop."

He pulled out a rather grimy handkerchief and blew his nose loudly. "Once they have exhausted our shop they are on to the next. Nothing better to do. I once suggested to one lady who had been in the shop over an hour that she become a volunteer. I might as well have suggested she abseiled down the side of the Shard!" He chuckled at his own joke.

She wondered how long he would carry on with his rather off-putting tales when a young man appeared from the back of the shop. He looked rather frazzled. On seeing her he weaved his way to the till through the customers. She put on her smile that she thought looked confident. There was an awkward moment when she thought he was going to shake her hand and brought hers up to meet his. However, he was merely scratching his head, a habit she would witness repeating itself during the afternoon. Embarrassed, she put her arm down by her side.

"So glad you could make it. We only spoke briefly the other day when you popped in. We have been very short of staff today but I am sure Alan is very capable of holding the fort whilst we go out the back for the induction talk, aren't you Alan?" Alan looked anything but, in fact, she thought, she would be surprised if Alan was still there on their return. She found herself following the young man, who she assumed was George Forbes, although he had not actually introduced himself. Dodging round the customers, she found herself in a room filled with boxes, clothes rails, towering piles of books and general organised chaos.

"Let's sit here and go through Health and Safety and Accident prevention Strategies. "It was obvious he had repeated these ad nauseum and the words tripped off his tongue without the necessity of looking at a pamphlet or brochure. It was all common sense to her and she gradually began to feel less apprehensive, allowing herself to relax a bit. She interjected with the odd "yes" and "I see" or "I can manage that" in the appropriate places. He sprung up at one point, like a jack in a box, returning with a pair of white rubber gloves. "These are to sort through the clothes with," he explained. "You would be horrified at the amount of dirty clothing we receive, even underwear." She inwardly recoiled at this, although it did not really surprise her at all. Some people's standards were very low.

He had sprung up again, returning this time with a gun, not the firearm type, she smiled to herself at the thought of that, but a clothes-labelling gun that thrust a spike through each item affixing a price tag to it. He demonstrated on a dress that had obviously been spiked on numerous occasions to explain the technique to new recruits. Well, that all seemed fairly simple. She was allowed to have a few trial spikes and eventually mastered the task, handing the gun back to George, who again was scratching his head, triumphantly.

Once again, she saw him catapulting from his seat returning with a curious object that she did not recognise. "The steam wand," he explained, "We hang up the suits, dresses, skirts and trousers and steam the creases out. A wonderful invention, saves all that tedious ironing." She attempted to put an expression of being truly impressed on her face. Well, perhaps she was, just a little bit.

Having finished the backroom induction talk, he guided her back to the shop floor and showed her how the clothing was hung on the rails, sized and grouped into colour ranges. She liked that. She appreciated order. She felt it was all straight forward and was about to say so when she realised George had made a bee line for the till. She quickly followed him. Here he went into intricate detail with accompanying head scratches, about the Gift Aid, Pink Stickers, World Cancer Day, stand up to Cancer Day and finally, with apologetic tones, introduced the topic of "shaking the bucket". This was a periodic stint of standing with a tin in the High Street collecting donations from often reluctant, over-busy pedestrians who had not quite perfected the ability to avoid eye contact. "It can be quite cold," he explained. "So we don't ask you to do it often," he quickly added.

"Would you like to start on the till or in the store room?" George had obviously finished the induction.

"The till please," she replied, "If you think I'd manage all right?"

"You won't know 'till' you try!" he roared with laughter at his own joke. She responded as well as she could with a short chuckle but her mind was already on the daunting task of being in sole charge of the incoming money. Alan had long since disappeared, having completed the morning shift, and she couldn't see any sign of the lady who had been filling shelves.

"Break a leg," shouted George as she watched his retreating back disappear into the stockroom. It wasn't until then that she realised that she still had her coat on and her handbag was still on her arm. Too embarrassed to call George back she put them both under the counter. "Needs must," she thought to herself.

Then she waited. She wondered how long it would be before she could test out her newly-acquired shop skills. There were six people altogether, roaming around, picking up pieces of memorabilia, reading the first chapter of a book, sifting through the CD and DVD rack, holding up clothes to the light or against their body for size. No movement towards the till though.

"Excuse me." She was shaken out of her reverie by a voice that seemed to come from nowhere. She then realised it was a child of about five years old whose head hardly rose above the height of the counter. "I want this," the voice continued.

She leaned over and extracted a large fluffy rabbit from the hands of the infant purchaser and was about to look at the price label attached to said animals ear, when a much larger hand extracted it from her grip removing the infant simultaneously. "She don't want that, little so and so, she can't keep her hands off anything. She's got too many toys as it is, 'er dad spoils 'er rotten." With that she strode out of the shop steering a now grizzling child in front of her.

She felt quite deflated. Her first sale and it turned out not to be a sale. Still, she put that down to beginner's bad luck.

"How much?" A strident voice matching a strident woman was standing at the counter. She pulled herself together. She examined the black gloves as the customer rummaged through her purse. She realised there was no price tag on them. Thinking on her feet she calculated how much the gloves would be worth. "£2.50 please. Is that O.K?" she ventured.

"Those are my bleeding gloves, this is what I am buying." The customer pushed a set of soaps in a box towards her from the place it had been positioned. Though she excused herself with the fact that it was further away than the gloves, it didn't make her feel any less stupid.

"Do you need a bag?" she asked.

"You flaming charge for them now don't you. Bleeding disgrace, if you ask me. No, I'll stick 'em in me 'andbag." At which she did exactly that, paid the required £1.50 and disappeared out of the shop.

She contemplated on this. One no-sale and one sale, eventually happening after her initial mistake. Not a brilliant record up to now. It could only get better surely.

She checked her watch. 3.35pm. Just under an hour to closing. Still no offer of a cup of tea. She was just weighing up the pros and cons of trying to locate George when a group of secondary school pupils pushed through the shop door and descended on the handbags.

"This all you've got?" one of them shouted across to her through a mouth of chewing gum, repositioning her school bag on her back.

She panicked. She didn't know if they had any more handbags or not. She would have to call for George.

"What is it you are looking for?"

"Don't know till I see 'em do I?"

She thought about this for a moment.

"I will ask if we have anything out the back. Won't be long."

She hurried into the storeroom and called George. He hurried out at a pace applicable to responding to a fire alarm.

"What is it? Is there something wrong?" His head scratching became quite manic. He seemed a bit irritable, which she thought was rather unfair as it was her first day.

She explained the situation to him. He eyed up the group of girls. "Only what you see on the shelves. We haven't priced and labelled the rest yet."

"Load of rubbish if you ask me," one of the girls exclaimed as she tossed a bag she was examining back on the pile. "Get one cheaper at Primark."

"Could I suggest you take your loud voices and rude remarks and go to Primark then!" She couldn't believe she had said it. Perhaps it was the tensions of the whole day getting the better of her. She blushed, not knowing quite what to do. Apologise?

"Oh charming!" This came from the gum chewer.

"Oh, come on Sophie, silly cow can do one!" one of the others shouted.

"We ain't coming in here again. Smells of sweaty

trainers anyway!" one of the others joined in.

At that they all left the shop as loudly as they had entered it.

Quite what "do one" meant she wasn't really sure and did not really want to find out. More important was the fact that George had been witness to her being dismissive of potential customers. This was her third failure on her first day. She felt quite despondent. She turned around expecting George to be scowling at the least, instead he was beaming from ear to ear.

"I have wanted to say something similar to those girls for months. They come in here about three times a week, demanding we go out the back to look for stock and disappear, probably with a good selection of the produce. I have never been able to catch them and I have never confronted them. Well done. Hopefully that's the last we shall see of them." He paused savouring the thought.

"Now how about I make you a nice cup of tea and you make yourself comfortable in the back room for ten minutes whilst you drink it. I will lock the doors and get ready to go. My bus is in twenty minutes but we have time for a quick chat."

Comfortable... She smiled at the use of her favourite word. So, feeling quite proud of herself that she had triumphed over the rude girls, she bent down to retrieve her handbag from under the counter.

The handbag wasn't there. She searched deeper under the counter with a sinking heart and a deflated self-esteem.

"Oh well," she thought, "those girls did find a handbag to suit them after all."

About the Author

Janet taught Drama and English for 35 years, directing a lot of plays, some of which she wrote herself. She has been spurred to start writing again having found a folder of poetry she had written over the years. She is now enjoying writing short stories with the aim of turning some of them into scripts. She feels she is at the start of an adventure and feels very excited about it.

Life Begins at the 250 Bus Stop
Jacqueline Ewers

Sweet tea

Autumn 2014

I push the key in the door. Kicking off my shoes, I head for the kitchen. Most nights I can't be bothered to make the effort to cook a proper meal. The microwave pings as my toast pops out of the toaster. I pour baked beans over brown bread. The smell is comforting. I settle down in front of the telly. The evening passes as I watch several episodes of *Say Yes to the Dress*. Getting ready for bed, I pull a long satin nightdress out of a drawer full of negligees. After slipping it on, I bundle up in a cardigan. I wouldn't be this cold if I had a husband to snuggle up to. I put socks on and slump beside my bed to pray. God, have you forgotten me?

I've been praying for a husband for years. I'm fed up of the repeated chorus 'I am praying God will send you a husband, Sister Maxine. Wait on the Lord and be of good courage.' Today was the worst. After Pastor Kendal's sermon: Don't Worry Your Boaz is Around the Corner, everyone came to encourage me. I wanted to tell them to bog off. God, why haven't you sent someone for me? It is so unfair. Disappointment climbs into bed with me. As I fill the empty space on my right with pillows, tears fall on the duvet cover.

We were a tight-knit church youth group until

members started getting married. It was great to begin with. Sometimes I was bridesmaid two or three times a year. But by twenty-eight, I was in the group of women no one chose to marry. By forty, friends stopped looking out for guys for me saying 'I was too picky'. Others said my 'lack of faith' was the reason I was still single.

I sit with Amanda in Tuesday night Prayer Meeting expecting the same routine; a few songs followed by prayer. Pastor Amy gives an exhortation entitled Trust God, Your Ram is in the Thicket with great animation and enthusiasm. Voices mingle as members respond to the message.

"Praise the Lord!"

"Hallelujah!"

Suddenly, Pastor Amy calls me to the altar. Sweat beads form on my upper lip as I try to avoid the glances of the others. Terrified, I make my way wondering what she's going to say. Pastor Amy shouts from the podium, "The Lord says you will be married within eighteen months."

Stunned, I lift my hands in praise. "Thank you God, finally you've heard my prayer."

The next evening while scrolling through my Facebook newsfeed, a notification pops up. Shiloh Church is holding a speed dating evening tomorrow. God, will I find him there? I register for the event.

The small church hall is decorated with clusters of red and white balloons with tables covered in contrasting red and white paper table covers. There's a low buzz of excited voices. I feel as if I have arrived late even though I am ten minutes early. Ten smartly dressed men casually discuss sport amongst themselves. I see nine impeccably presented women clustered in groups of three. They seem to know each other. I note their smiles fixed in place to catch the eye of a potential mate. I approach one group saying, "Hello." Heat rises to my face as I sense their scrutiny. I'm so glad I changed into something smart before leaving work. A bell rings. The room becomes quiet. A fifty something woman introduces herself as Sister Yvonne. Her hair is swept back in a simple pony tail and her face is make-up free. She prays to open the evening asking for God's direction.

"Ladies and gentlemen, when you came in you were given a number. Please sit at that table. The bell will ring after 10 minutes. Gentlemen, you will then move onto the next table in a clockwise direction."

I am quickly bored with number one. He only speaks about his Lexus car. On close inspection number two has pencilled in his eyebrows. A definite no. Number three just quotes scripture the whole time. Number four, doesn't make eye contact. I think he's a bit shifty rather than shy. The fleshy gaps between the straining buttons of Number five's shirt put me off. Six makes it clear that he is the centre of his world. Seven is looking for a woman to replace his mother. Eight becomes uninterested when I say I don't like football.

Nine is Pete. Our conversation flows with ease. He's a Pentecostal. Tick. Working. Tick. Funny. Tick. Looking for a wife. Huge tick. God is this him?'I don't really engage with Number ten because I'm thinking about Pete. The final bell rings. Some men duck for the door, while others linger. I quickly look at my phone pretending not to notice Pete coming towards me.

"Hey Maxine, you fancy grabbing something to eat tomorrow evening?"

"Yeah, why not?" I say, trying to mask my excitement. He gives me his number and we arrange to meet at Tooting Bec Station at 8pm. "Thank you Jesus, I didn't expect to meet my husband so soon." I sing *God my provider* all the way home, fantasising about my wedding.

It takes me all day to get ready. I choose an outfit to show off my figure. Hair freshly styled, flawless Mac face, I head out for Tooting. The thrill of dating bubbles away feeding my excitement. "I can't believe I've found him already. Thank you Lord."

"Hey Maxi, you look great."

"Thanks, where are we are we going?"

"Oh, it's not far."

We chat chirpily as we walk down the road. "We're here," he announces. My breath catches in my throat. As we go inside, the Chicken Cottage menu looms over me. He throws the words "'Dutch yeah?" over his shoulder at me, and then places his order. Not wanting to look as if I can't pay for my meal, I order a wrap and a drink. I watch him shovel a handful of chips in his mouth. As he talks about himself, bits of chips fall to the table. He absentmindedly picks them up putting them in his mouth. *This cannot be the one, no bloody way.* I try to be pleasant but when the chicken fat runs down his chin dripping onto the table, I get up mumbling something about feeling sick and leave. Deflated, wondering about the promise of a husband, I make my way home, blocking his number.

Spring 2015

As I brown the meat, the spicy curry powder, mingled with ginger and garlic waft throughout my flat promising a tasty meal. Rice simmers away releasing its buttery aroma. It's been so long since I cooked a proper meal. Amanda chops cucumber.

"Did you hear? Marj is pregnant."

"No way."

"Because she's single she'll have to give up her post as Sunday School Superintendent. Such a shame, she loves those kids."

"Now she'll finally have one of her own. I know what it's like to be sick of being the godmother and never the mother. Do you think she did it on purpose?"

"Who knows?... I blame our church rules; no sex before marriage; no co-habitation; no marrying non-Christians. I feel smothered."

"This purity thing ain't easy."

"Well, I got myself a rubber friend to keep me company." Amanda confesses as she sips her wine.

"What you saying to me? You know that's a no-no."

"What's a girl to do?"

"I'm keeping myself pure for my husband." I say, not mentioning crying many nights wondering where he is.

"You do just that. God is faithful. The prophecy will come to pass."

We continue chatting during our meal. I savour every mouthful. I had forgotten how much I love my own cooking and eating with company. After Amanda leaves I wash up the dishes mulling over my secret encounter with Brother Barry.

Winter 2014

I first noticed him visiting in a Sunday morning service three months ago. His smooth baritone voice caught my attention. I admired his dapper look and fudge-coloured skin. "God, is this him?" I approached him striking up a conversation. His *Paul Smith* aftershave gently tickled my nostrils. He became a regular visitor. "Can I have your number?" he asked one day. "I just want to check you get home safely." No guy had ever bothered about my safety before.

"Yes of course."

He was charming. I felt special and valued.

"That colour on your nails accentuates your beautiful long fingers."

"That scarf you're wearing looks fantastic. It compliments your eyes."

Our dates were incredible. Tea at The Shard and Cocktails at Maxwell's. A far cry from Chicken Cottage. I loved being a couple. "Please God let this be the one." I subscribe to *Wedding Magazine*.

"Let's not tell anyone we're dating just yet. It's much more exciting."

"OK," I said wondering why.

After a while, he asked if he could spend the night at my flat. When I said no, he ignored my calls and messages. A week later I decided to go to his house. I rang the doorbell. When he opened the door I confronted him.

"Why are you ignoring me?"

"As you're here, come in. I know what you need." he said reaching for my breasts.

"For God's sake B. Stop it." I knock his hand away.

"Max, I don't know why you're carrying on like your fanny is paved with gold and lined with diamonds. I should be able get me some sex anytime, I've earned it. Those dates were investments; it's payback time."

"If it wasn't for the grace of God, I would cuss out your backside." He slams the door in my face. I kick the door shouting, "Arsehole."

I was furious, mostly at myself. I can't believe I imagined us walking down the aisle. I found out later that Barry had slept with a couple of my single friends at church. Now, I'm glad it was only my temper I lost with the bugger. Drying the dishes I ask, "God, was the prophecy really a word from you?"

Spring 2015

On my way to buy hard dough bread and bun, this guy walks up to the 250 bus stop, T-shirt exposing toned muscles. His eyes are a striking caramel against his rich chestnut skin. I fancy him straight away.

"You been waiting long?" he says smiling.

"Only a few minutes."

"Happy Easter. I'm on my way to Brixton for bun and bread. I can imagine the queue when I get there. I hope the bus comes soon."

"I'm going to the bakery too… sorry for being forward but you sound Jamaican." The bus arrives, I get on first.

"Yes, I grew up there but came back to London a while ago. Have you been?"

"My parents used to take me when I was younger. Beautiful island." I'm chuffed when he sits next to me. As we chat about Jamaican Easter traditions, I check his wedding finger. Empty. I think to hell with it and ask for his number.

"Amanda, I've met this guy. We've been dating for a few weeks now."

"Really? I can't believe you've kept him a secret."

"I wanted to see if things would work out. Guess what? He's a Jamaican minister."

"Shut… up, a minister."

"I know right. He's Baptist, but he's sweet like condensed milk. Pray he's the one."

He makes a mean steam snapper, stuffed with okra, and callaloo steeped in butter. Oh my word, when I ate the fish I embarrassed myself. It was so tasty I sucked the juice from the fish head. We talk about Jamie for the next two hours.

Daily I pray, "God let him be the one." Dating is fun. It's the first time I've felt loved: Surprise flowers at work, and unexpected gifts. We laugh comparing the similarities and differences between Jamaican and Black British culture. I'm constantly learning something new. I look forward to our evenings together which always end in prayer.

Autumn 2015

"What's up? It's the middle of the night?" Amanda answers her phone sleepily.

"Sorry, I know it's late but I can't wait till morning… I'm engaged."

"Max. That's fantastic! Tell me everything. How did he ask? What's your ring like?"

"This evening we went to watch the World Championship athletics. Jamie asked me to marry him just after Usain Bolt won his last race. Fans were standing cheering, chanting and waving the Jamaican flag. The atmosphere was electric. It took me two seconds to say yes. My ring is platinum with green and white diamonds. So beautiful. I can't believe I'm finally getting married. I'm too excited to sleep, you coming over?"

"I'll be there in half an hour."

When she arrives we squeal, drink champagne, dance around and tumble down giggling like little girls.

When Pastor Kendal announces my engagement, brethren dance in the aisles praising God for answered prayers and the fulfilment of the prophecy. Some older sisters struggle to move their arthritis-ridden bodies so bang their walking sticks on the carpet.

Spring 2016

Today, is the final fitting for my dress. The sweetheart neckline trimmed with scalloped lace emphasises my bust line. The shimmering diamanté crystals and beads on the bodice hug my body. My image takes my breath away. I run my hand over the weighty satin of the skirt, such a luxurious feel. "Jamie will be over the moon when he sees you. You look breathtaking." Amanda says.

"You expect me to leave my church after over thirty years Jamie?" I shout, no regard for others in the coffee shop.

"Yes, of course. You know it's tradition. I want

you to serve with me in my church."

"Why can't you serve at my church?"

"Maxine, stop your stupidness. I want you by my side as my wife at home and in ministry. If you can't do that then it's simple, you're not ready to be my wife. Let me know what you decide." He walks out the door.

I wrestle, wondering am I ready for marriage, to compromise and give up some of my independence? Do I have what it takes to leave the church I know so well despite its flaws?

"You look dreadful. Bags under your eyes, hair matted together. What's going on?" Amanda enquires.

"Jamie's expects me to join his church after we're married. I'm scared of change. I haven't slept properly or been out for days."

"Are you out of your mind? You knew all along you would have to go to his church. It's tradition. You would pass up marrying Jamie for what exactly? He really does love you, even the blind can see that. Look at all the times he's put your choices first. Fix up Maxine, stop being selfish. Call Jamie and tell him you'll follow him to his church. After all, you two belong together."

As we sign the marriage certificate, Jamie declares, "You're the answer to my prayers. I love you Mrs Thomas."

Winter 2016

I love being Jamie's wife. We're both getting used to married life. It's been good. I'm quite settled in his church now. The members are really nice to me. I hardly see the old youth group but Amanda keeps me up to date on our nights out. It's funny, Jamie really did turn out to be my unexpected 'ram in the thicket'.

About the author:
The Secret by Jacqueline Robinson is available from Amazon.

On Time

Lisa Williams

A double brandy

The scream ceased after sixty-seven seconds. The memory of it went on forever for all those that heard it.

The precise moment it began her life ended. As she watched her only child rise up into the air. Like the weightless astronaut he dreamt of being.

Those dreams finished then with the dull bump that shattered the windscreen. The thud they all relived over and over. If only she hadn't shouted for him to hurry up. If just once she'd let him be late. Then her thoughts turned to sobs and she crumpled in a heap on the pavement.

About the author
Lisa is predominantly a writer of short stories and particularly likes the tight word constraint of a drabble. She's a cheery soul but you wouldn't guess that from her writing as she often dwells on the darker sides of life. Lisa has fully embraced social media and can be found as @noodleBubble on most platforms.

Redemption

Richard Hough

Hot chocolate with all the trimmings

Ruby had never forgiven herself for what happened on that August day and had finally found a way to make amends.

She reflected on the "accident" and how it had changed so many lives. Why did her Nan get so close to the cess pit in the first place?

"Come and have a look at this dear," the old woman called out. Ruby couldn't imagine what there was to see but Nan was always showing her things in the woods when they went out for walks. The old lady knew the names of all the flowers and birds and Ruby loved how Nan treated them all with respect.

Ruby was always a clumsy child. It was a bit of a family joke and somehow made her feel special. As she leaned over to see what Nan had spotted, she accidentally nudged the old lady who was only six stones wet through. Nan lost her balance quickly disappearing into the dark, disgusting sludge in the hole usually hidden under the metal guard. Frozen with terror, Ruby tried to scream for help but no sound came out.

"Is everything alright?" The deep voice made her jump. It was one of the wolf family who lived deeper in the woods. They often popped along to see Nan, bringing her the occasional venison steak.

"F… f… fine, th… th… thank you," she sniffed, tears running freely down her cheeks.

At that moment Ruby's father arrived after a day working in the woods. He was part of the team which managed the large area of forest trying to keep the balance of nature exactly as it should be.

"Hello Ruby what have you been up to?"

Ruby saw a chance to save herself and without further thought of consequences cried out, "Oh Daddy, please help, the wolf has eaten Nanny."

"Now hold on. I've just arrived," insisted the wolf, nonplussed.

The woodsman ran into the house but could find no trace of his elderly mother. Believing Ruby to be a truthful child, he picked up his axe and without further questions, took the second innocent life that day.

Now, twenty years later, Ruby stood outside the cage. The storm raged around her as she beckoned to the wolf. The family had been caged ever since the day of the 'accident'.

"Torak," she yelled, "over here."

"Who are you?" demanded the elderly wolf.

"My name is Ruby, I… knew your grandfather."

"Wait a minute, I know who you are. You're the reason my grandfather was killed and why we're all in this prison."

"I'm so sorry. I had no idea what would happen. I was young and scared and it all happened so quickly. I've come to let you out. I want to put things right."

Ruby swung open the gate. "You're free again."

"I've waited a long time for revenge," snarled Torak, uttering the last words Ruby would ever hear.

Having devoured the last of the woman, Torak headed into the Berkshire countryside, ignoring the herds of sheep he passed.

About the author
Richard Hough still has nowhere to call home though he has bought a new shed (not from the profits of writing – still negligible). He was one of the authors in *The Best of CaféLit 7*. Richard has also written a new book and is looking for a publisher who is equally as strange as he is with a dark sense of humour - any suggestions welcome.

The Art Critic
Allison Symes

Cranberry and raspberry tea

The fairy took one look at the concrete monstrosity of a statue put up to represent Tinkerbell and blasted it to smithereens with a quick twitch of her wand. It was bad enough humans didn't really believe in fairy kind anymore but there was no way she would tolerate such a horrible depiction of the noblest of the magical species. So she didn't and considered it the finest piece of critical art analysis ever seen on Earth. It was just a shame she couldn't boast about it.

Very few would believe in her to believe her at all. She wished she could change that and teach humans to respect their betters. She wasn't allowed to grant her own wishes. It would be chaos she was told. She sighed. What it would've been was fun! But then fairies weren't supposed to indulge in that either, or so she'd been told.

She smiled. There was a lot the authorities didn't know despite all their magical capabilities. If folk were determined to do something, they'd find a way. It was one of the few things she understood about humanity given they shared the same trait. And now time to clear off and leave people wondering what happened to "their" Tinkerbell.

The fairy vanished. The very sharp of hearing might have just heard a slight laugh on the breeze as she did so.

About the author

Allison Symes writes fairytales with bite as flash fiction, novels and short stories. Her flash fiction collection, *From Light to Dark and Back Again*, was published by Chapeltown Books in 2017. She is a member of the Association of Christian Writers and Society of Authors. She adores P.G.Wodehouse, Jane Austen and Terry Pratchett. Allison's main website is www.fairytaleswithbite.weebly.com and she blogs for *Chandler's Ford Today* at http://chandlersfordtoday.co.uk/author/allison-symes/

Index Of Drinks

Write for CaféLit

What we want

We're looking for thought-provoking and entertaining stories, though ones which might be a tad different from what you normally read in a woman's magazine. They should be the sort of length that would make easy reading while you drink a cup of coffee, even if you linger a while, but without you needing to rent a table.

So, perhaps, no more than 3000 words. Shorter stories and flash fiction are naturally very welcome.

How to submit

Send your submission to gill@cafelit.co.uk. It should be in the body of the email. Please put "CafeLit Submission" in the subject line.

What happens next

We'll read your story. If we like it and plan to publish it we'll let you know, and if we don't like it we'll let you know. If your story fits our imprint and is of publishable quality we will keep it in an archive. If you manage to place your story elsewhere, please let us know the title and the day you submitted and we'll remove it from the archive. Normally, stories are published or rejected within a month, but sometimes we have a surge or a dearth in submissions.

Each day we publish the best of the day's submissions. If we have no submissions on a particular day we'll look in the archive and pick a particular story we like.

We usually schedule stories a few days in advance. This helps us to guarantee a daily story.

If your story is very seasonal, we'll schedule if for a particular date or time of year.

Author compensation

Each year we'll publish a volume of "The Best of" which will be sold as a trade book If you are in the volume you will have a share of the net sales. .

You may advertise yourself in a 50 word bio, including your web site details, if your story is over 1,000 words. If it is shorter, you still may include a link to your website. Both will be displayed at the end of your story. Our editing process will include some work on your bio to maximise its effect.

Copyright issues

By submitting and accepting our editing process you are indicating that you are willing to let CaféLit publish your work.

Copyright remains with you and you are free to publish your story elsewhere. Do check with any other publisher, however, that they are happy that we are also publishing your work. We like to keep your work on our pages for at least 365 days. After that, it will still stay there unless you ask us to remove it. We do ask, however, that you let us display your work for a year.

Something Quirky

Each story will be assigned the name of a drink. Something light and frothy might be a hot chocolate. A dark piece of flash fiction could be an espresso. Something good for the soul would be a mint tea.

You may assign your story a drink. We reserve the right to alter the assignment.

The Vision

During the Spring Forward night some years ago I did not sleep, but I did have a dream. My mind raced. The hunters have hunted and the gatherers have gathered and it is time to be around the camp-fire and drum, tell stories, sing, dance and make music and pictures.

Every town should have at least one Creative Café. They would be good at airports too. Ideally, everyone in the world should be within an hour of a Creative Café.

These are cafés where anyone can go to drink coffee, eat cakes and other such, a little in the way that the Viennese coffee houses used to operate. These may also be licensed so a glass of wine may be an option. There people can meet to discuss creative ideas or just soak up the creative ideas of others. Typically, writers meet to share writing and experiences. Artists display their work where the café area doubles us as a gallery. A shop may be present to sell creatively-produced items, items produced by the famous and the less-well-known as appropriate to each location.

Less conventional forms of creativity are also made welcome, and the visitors are not those actively engaged in creative activities. The atmosphere in the places fosters creative activity.

Location is important. Where Creative Cafés are

found in a university town, they are available for town and gown, and not out of sight of the public, hidden on a university campus.

Some are cafés that are already there and have taken on this creative activity. Others are purpose-made and, typically, they are in converted chapels, old barns, converted mills, or state of the art modern buildings. Conversions will be tastefully done, in an environmentally-friendly way. Getting it right is more important than money, though no one's business should suffer because of it, and may even benefit indirectly financially because of added value. There is no formula – each one suits its location. Often the catering is local and creatively in-keeping.

Events may take place there – poetry readings, book launches, viewings of art and sculpture, soap-boxing of creative solutions, theatre performances, film screenings, recitals, exhibitions, concerts, conventional or less conventional – at any time of the day, in keeping with local cultures. As well as any event taking place, there is free access for like-minded people who wish to meet together. Some events are free, some events make a charge to cover costs, and some aim to make a profit – for a particular cause or to further promote the work of the Creative Café Project. Some events will have a fixed-price charge. Some will ask for a donation.

Arts councils and states may support the cafés, but they will not control them. They belong to the people, but the people are entrepreneurial and move towards the highest high, rather than sinking to the lowest low. The aim is the celebration of creativity. They outshine the French "Maison de la Culture" and are less eccentric than the French "salon".

Whoever manages the cafés, at local, national or international level, has good business skills. The main brief is to keep the cafés vibrant and running effectively. This includes taking account of finances, but not to make huge profits, unless, for an individual café, it seems appropriate to support some cause or help other cafés to get up and running, or needing itself major refurbishments or expansion.

Any café can join the project and there is no fee to pay. This web site acts as a platform for informing the world about where these cafes exist. The project aims to enhance the experience of those who visit the creative cafés.

Also By Chapeltown Books

www.ingramcontent.com/pod-product-compliance
Lightning Source LLC
Chambersburg PA
CBHW071344170626

46811CB00003B/984